SON OF OSIVIRIUS

CATHRYN DEVRIES

PRAISE FOR 'SON OF OSIVIRIUS'

"Delicious world building and characters that sparkle with agency. *Son of Osivirius* deftly highlights the importance of the natural world and humanity's place within it. Cathryn deVries weaves a brilliant tale." — Pamela Jeffs, *Aurealis Award winner and author of Wilder*

"A lushly imagined, and hopeful serving of adventure filled with heart, humanity and flying cats. I loved it!" — Trent Jamieson, *award-winning author of Stone Road, Day Boy, the Death Works Series, and the Nightbound Land Duology*

"I adored this story from start to finish. A gripping plot, believable characters, and a richly immersive world that overflows with imagination and compassion." — Kylie Chan, *best-selling author of the Dark Heavens series and the Dragon Empire series*

"*Son of Osivirius* is a beautiful story of what it means to truly be content. Filled with relatable characters who fight only to live in peace, this book is the perfect read for anyone looking for a deeply satisfying story of adventure, love, and destiny." — Hannah Gaudette, *author of the Destined Duology and the One Light Trilogy*

"This story is a rousing, captivating adventure, full of thought-provoking themes and tantalizing romance!" — Kathryn Jordan, *author of the Keeper of Light Series and The Wolf Warden*

"Creating a great new world with a story of trust and love, *Son of Osivirius* is a stunning new science fantasy that I can't recommend enough." — Stephen Hipkiss, *fantasy author and director of Hipkiss Publishing House*

"*Son of Osivirius* is a unique story set in a lush world with original world building that fans of Avatar will enjoy." — Jemma Pollari, *fantasy author and director of the Spec Fic Society*

"*Son of Osivirius* brings Avatar-style adventure to a new and interesting world!" — Addison Horner, *author of The Vitalian Chronicles, editor, and director of Avocado Tree Press*

"*Son of Osivirius* is an immersive and rewarding read for fans of science fantasy who appreciate rich world building, thoughtful themes, and characters who feel genuinely invested in the world they are trying to protect." —*Next Best Read*

"*Son of Osivirius* surprised me with its heart. Beneath the adventure and the danger, this is a story about belonging and trust, and how hard it is to let go of fear in order to live freely. I would recommend this book to readers who enjoy science fiction that balances action with deeper themes, especially fans of *Avatar* or *The Left Hand of Darkness*. It's also a great pick for anyone who wants an adventure with strong characters, a lush setting, and deep ideas." —*Literary Titan*

"Overall, a beautifully crafted novel and a compelling read for young adults. With superb world building, captivating characters, and a tender slow-burn romance, this is a must read for fans of dystopian science fiction and fantasy." —*Readers Choice*

SON OF OSIVIRIUS

CATHRYN DEVRIES

Edited by Alice Sudlow and Kim Smith

Book Cover by 100 Covers

Interior formatting and chapter graphics by Catherine Nohlmans

ISBN 978-1-7641667-1-3 (paperback)

ISBN 978-1-7641667-2-0 (hardcover)

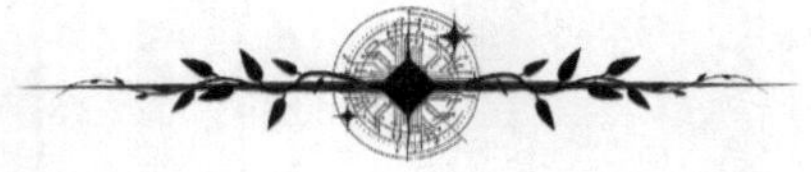

To Mother Earth,
who has taught me so much,
and withholds nothing from her children,
like the one who created her.

Chapter 1

Jayden

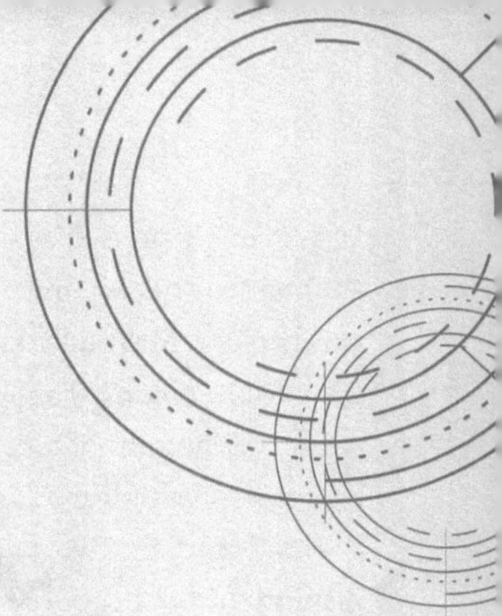

PAIN. PAIN AND BLACKNESS. The taste of blood in my mouth. My first awareness centred on these. Half-dazed, I registered that someone had removed my helmet, then fingers pressed on my neck, checking for a pulse. A concerned voice—masculine—broke through my stupor.

"The pilot's still alive. Whadda we do?"

The words bounced around in my skull, not really making sense. Then a second voice—feminine—answered his question.

"Kill him. They'll assume he died in the crash." The tone was flat, business-like.

With dawning terror, I froze.

Rebels. Rebels had found me.

"I never pegged you as *that* heartless, sis."

I couldn't breathe. Couldn't think. *What do I do? What do I do? Dammit! How did this even happen?*

"We have to think of what's best for everyone, and seriously, would you expect them to spare us if they found us?"

There was a pause as the guy considered her question—and my training took over.

No time for pain. I had to think.

Ok. No sudden moves. Keep my eyes closed. Pretend I can't hear them.

"No... probably not."

Not the answer I was hoping for.

Pain coursed through my legs, my arms, my ribs, and the humid

Osivirian air pressed against me now that my cabin was broached. But I remained still, willing them to just leave me for dead. Maybe nothing was broken. Maybe I could limp out of here and signal for an evac. Get back to the colony. To my family...

At the thought of what might happen to them if I didn't come back, an extra spike of fear added itself to the already nightmarish situation.

Beside me, the two were silent, then I heard some movement, a slight rasping sound, heavy breathing.

"C'mon, do it while he's still unconscious."

Terror constricted every part of me, and my eyes flew open to see a dagger hovering only inches away.

I jerked back, fire igniting in every muscle. A horrible sound escaped my mouth, then, "No, please!"

I seized the eyes of the guy, then his sister, then the guy again, mine so wide that they hurt. I think I was gasping, staying alive all I could think of.

The guy lowered the dagger.

His sister huffed. "Fine, give it to me. I'll do it. You can knock him out if it makes you feel better."

I started shaking.

"Please," I said again, my pained voice barely above a whisper.

The guy jerked the dagger out of the girl's reach, sheathing it. "No. I'm not doing it. Besides, maybe we can learn something from him."

"Or create a mass of complications," the girl said in a caustic tone.

"I don't care," he snapped. "I'm not taking his life, and neither are you." He turned to me. "Where's it hurt?"

I saw his sister roll her eyes and stand upright, hands on hips, and with the immediate danger withdrawn, took in some more details. She looked in her early twenties, same as me, some Asian heritage revealed in her smooth, dark hair and almond eyes. Both she and her brother wore fatigues of deep green—the colour of the foliage here—with a dagger strapped to her thigh and sleeves rolled up. Very much like colony soldiers.

I remained wary as I turned back to the guy. "Everywhere."

A frown creased his forehead. "Nettle, bring a stretcher team and Doc Aspen," he said, then turned back to me. "I'm a medic. I'll do what I can for you till the doc gets here. I'll need to feel for breaks, ok? Your 'thopter came down hard. We weren't expecting to find you alive."

As he undid my harness and rummaged around in a pouch, I vaguely recalled the controls going haywire, the altimeter spinning the wrong way as the FCS tried to correct what it thought was an out-of-control spiral—with an out-of-control spiral. I remembered battling with the manual controls; over-correcting. There were red lights flashing, sirens blaring, greenery coming ever closer...

A pungent rag smothered my face and I reflexively struggled... then blackness returned.

Chapter 2
Nettle

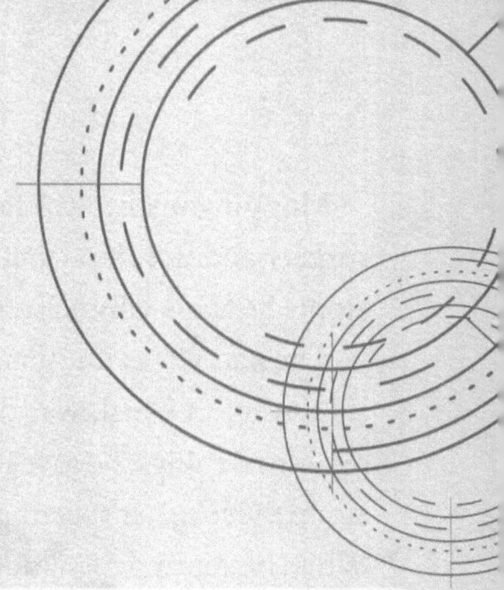

I stood on the wide ledge in front of the Masu den, watching for the first of the salvage crews to crest the ridgeline. At last, a net with its two accompanying Masu appeared.

"Right, here they come!" called Grandma Lily to those of us in the assembled sorting crews. "You have your assignments. Let's make this turnaround as quick as possible!"

Crouching with the rest of my team, I sprang forward as the salvage crew lowered the load of 'thopter parts onto the ledge and began running pieces to their designated collection points. Baskets began to fill with tubing, circuit boards and plastics, and mounds of metal, plexiglass and carbon fibre quickly grew too. This was a brilliant score, as we could use all of these things, but we were particularly low on metal. It was lucky Flint and I had seen the 'thopter go down.

Excited chatter amongst other nearby sorters drew my attention.

"It's quite mangled, isn't it?"

"I heard the pilot survived."

"How could anyone survive a crash like this?"

"Don't know, but he did."

"Might still die of his injuries."

"Maybe, but what if he doesn't?"

"Guess we wait and see."

Their questions got me thinking again. 'Thopter *parts* might be extremely useful, but a 'thopter *pilot* certainly wasn't. I grumbled as I ran another panel over to a mound. Flint's soft heart would lead to trouble down the line.

Mopping my brow, I raised my eyes to the section of caves where the surgery and hospital facilities were located, and saw Doc coming down alone. Strange, why wasn't Flint with him?

The nets were almost empty now, and Doc checked in with Grandma Lily, who, as usual, was directing operations. After hearing how she'd organised things, he gave his wife a brief kiss and squeeze, and wandered along the ledge, inspecting the piles and encouraging people as he went. When he spotted me, smile lines crinkled around his eyes, and he headed over.

"Where's Flint?" I asked before he could say anything.

"I left him to monitor the pilot."

Something inside me became very uncomfortable at this, but I tried to keep my expression neutral. "Why? There are nursing staff who could do that."

Doc tilted his head and hummed; gave me his 'Really, Nettle?' look. "Perhaps, but it's important he learns what signs to look for, and practices taking readings. Besides, he was eager. He's shaping up to be a fine doctor."

I grunted. "Too good." Lifting the final piece of metal from my assigned net, I stepped back so the crew could take off again.

Doc put a hand on my arm. "What's wrong, Nettle? You seem worried about something."

I stilled, met his gaze. "Of course I'm worried about something. There's a flaming Central pilot in our valley. Why *wouldn't* I be worried?"

"Because he's severely injured and isn't a threat to anyone?"

"But he's *here*. That in itself is a huge problem." Pulling my arm out of his grip, I strode over to the appropriate pile and dumped my piece in it.

Doc followed me. "We don't know that yet."

I straightened, put my hands on my hips. "Please tell me he's going to be a prisoner."

Doc sighed. "This needs more discussion."

"What's to discuss?" I demanded. "He's an enemy soldier."

Doc narrowed his eyes. "The people of the colony are not our enemies, Nettle."

"Somehow I don't think they feel the same way."

"Be that as it may, this is the first 'thopter that's come anywhere near us, we have the black box and the beacon, and we are well protected here. It was pure luck that you and Flint were on your way home from zone-5 and saw him."

Doc had a point, but my hatred ran too deep. I lowered my gaze. "Doesn't mean he shouldn't be a prisoner."

Sighing again, Doc put his hands on both of my shoulders. "Nettle, I love you dearly, my girl, but you can't keep feeding your anger like this. It's not healthy." He gently took my chin between one thumb and forefinger and lifted it. "You're safe. We're safe. I made sure of that."

I shrugged him off. "But for how much longer?"

Again, Doc sighed. "This pilot is no threat. He won't even be able to walk for weeks. Please, trust me. Trust the leadership team."

It didn't seem like I had much choice.

But Doc had led us well these past fifteen years, always knowing what to do next, and keeping everyone's spirits up when things were the hardest. He and Grandma Lily had adopted me and Flint, made room for us even though they had hundreds of other people to look after. I owed him this much.

"Fine. But I'm not going to let my guard down."

Chapter 3

Jayden

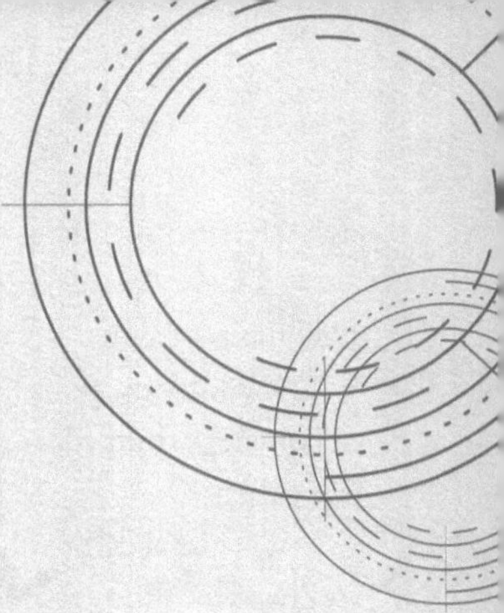

"**I** STILL THINK WE should've killed him."

Nettle's voice roused me from semi-consciousness. My fear ignited immediately; any lingering brain fog shattered in the ice of her words.

But where was I? What was happening? I took a mental inventory of my body. It didn't take long: I ached all over. Through the discomfort, I registered I was lying on a thin mattress, and all of my limbs were immobilised.

Trapped. I was trapped.

Breathing shallow, I blinked my eyes into focus. The room, if it *was* a room, was dim, and mats of woven palm shielded my view of Nettle and whomever she was speaking to. A sweet, herbaceous scent floated on the air, but it did nothing to calm me.

"Well, I'm glad we didn't." The brother's voice. "This way we have a bargaining chip."

Bargaining chip...

The fear loosened a fraction. I was a hostage. I could work with 'hostage'.

"What makes you think they'll care enough to want him back, Flint?" Nettle demanded. "It's not like he was carrying any valuable cargo, and no one means anything to them. Everyone is just a number in the system; a cog in the machine. We escaped that. Why risk even contacting them?"

"Maybe they'll leave us alone."

"For *one* pilot? You're trippier than Vine."

"Maybe. Or maybe I'm just tired of hiding," Flint said with a weary sigh. "Returning him as an act of goodwill might show them—"

"—That we're weak. That we need them." Nettle's voice was scathing.

Flint was silent.

The knot loosened a little more. They didn't know why I was here.

Footsteps shuffled, and a new voice entered the conversation. "How's our patient?"

"I was just about to check on him, Doc."

That was Flint, and his tone kicked my brain fully into gear. His naivety could be useful, and I *had* to escape this place.

Rustling indicated they were all walking towards me. Heart suddenly thumping again, I closed my eyes. At the sound of the mats being moved, I rocked my head from side to side and pretended to blink my eyes open. I didn't want them to suspect I'd overheard their conversation. Way too dangerous.

Light from the entrance silhouetted three figures: Nettle, Flint, and—I presumed—Doc Aspen.

"Ah, you're awake. You're lucky to be alive, young man, you know that?" Doc Aspen's voice was a curious mixture of light and matter-of-fact. I didn't know what to make of it.

Behind him, Nettle gave a snort. "Luckier than he knows," she muttered.

Flint elbowed her and lowered his brows, and Doc Aspen took a seat next to my bed.

I flicked my eyes between them all, not sure where I should look. Finally, I settled on Doc Aspen. "I... yes." I had to force the words past my dry throat.

Doc Aspen turned to Flint. "Some water and a straw, please."

"Sure, Doc."

While Flint stepped away, I took in the doctor's features. Deep creases lined the tanned skin of his face, and his hair was almost white. He wore thick glasses over his pale, blue eyes, but nothing else marked him as a doctor.

He turned back to me. "Do you have a name, young man? Do you remember what happened?"

I startled at the words, and didn't want to answer right away, but Flint returned with the water, so I took a grateful draw, then deliberately slowed to give myself time to think. These were rebels, and at least one of them wanted to kill me. Would it be dangerous to give them my real name? Did they have covert agents in the colony who would threaten my family? Whatever I told them, it certainly couldn't be the whole truth. It seemed I would be allowed to live for the moment, but who knew when that would change.

I saw Nettle glaring at me. If it was up to her, very soon.

I shifted my eyes to Flint, then the doctor. They acted nice now, but it might be a ruse. I couldn't take the chance, but neither would I blow this opportunity to lull them into complacency. I didn't risk taking this mission just to find myself helpless again.

My insides twisted. No, I would *never* let myself be that helpless again.

But, wrapped up like a mummy, subject to their whims, my best shot lay in making them *believe* I was harmless. It had worked plenty of times before.

"My name's Jayden," I said, putting on a kind of dazed and innocent look. "And... not really. I was just on a routine survey mission..."

Doc Aspen frowned. "Central put you in a lot of danger sending you near a dead-zone, Jayden. The electromagnetic barrier is ruinous to electronics. That's why we came here."

'Here' was one of the many 'Bermuda Triangle' black-spots of Osivirius, the planet we'd colonised only a generation ago. I was planet-born, and that had made me stupid enough to think I had some kind of innate ability to defeat the random electromagnetic eruptions that plagued it. Like a small number of other pilots, I'd been able to anticipate and handle them elsewhere, but what I'd encountered here hadn't been an eruption, it'd been a wall, its blanket strength ludicrous.

The number of dead-zones had been steadily increasing each year, spreading like cancer and wreaking havoc on our equipment. Central was sure the rebels were behind it. Colony Commander Tun wanted them brought under control, so had offered a huge reward for the location of their base—which had proven impossible to find. Like Doc Aspen said, every piece of tech became useless in these regions. Even satellite images turned into worthless pixelated murals. It was like there was some kind of interference barrier over every one of these areas. For this mission, I was just supposed to get a visual, then return. Instead, I'd accidentally infiltrated.

Feigning ignorance, I again tested the waters. "You're the rebels, aren't you?" I croaked. "The ones who abandoned the colony?"

Doc Aspen sighed and shook his head; looked off to the side. "A generation from now, we will be its salvation."

Salvation? What the heck was he on about?

It didn't matter.

One thing was certain though. When I got out of here, they would certainly be my *family's* salvation.

Chapter 4

Nettle

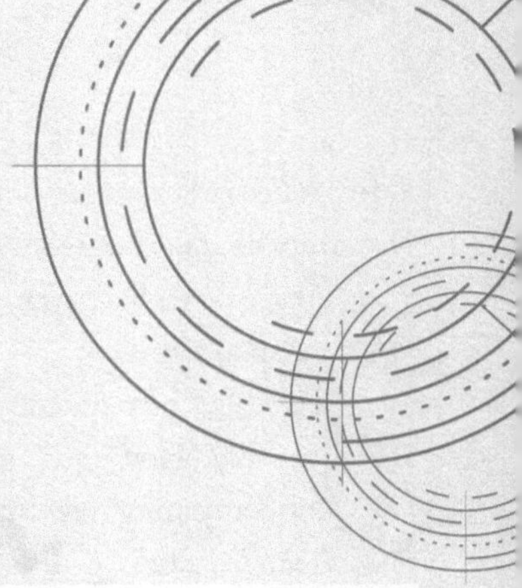

With a satisfied smile, I put my morning's work—a basket of new botanic samples—on my workbench in the lab. The lab and surgery caves were the most well-lit, with glass skylights set into the ceiling. Glass was something I was grateful we could produce. With it, I could continue my parents' work, studying the plant life of Osivirius. Somehow, Doc Aspen had managed to smuggle out a few decent microscopes and several boxes of slides, but the ability to manufacture more reassured me.

I walked over to the stone basin set into the wall and twisted a lever. Cold water streamed from a wooden pipe and over my hands. I soaped them up, washed to my elbows, then shut off the lever. The wastewater would end up in a swampy area to be naturally filtered, while the clean water piped from the waterfall was returned to the lake. I was proud of the system, for I'd discovered the hollow-tubed plants the pipes were made from shortly after I'd arrived here in the valley as a seven-year-old. The engineers had seen their potential immediately. They'd taken over from that point, but I still thought of them as *my* pipes.

Drying my hands, I headed for the 'bakery'—a mixture of clay and reflective solar ovens that were just about ready to deliver up fresh flatbread for lunch. Flint was sure to be on his way there too.

A darker mood descended. I was worried about him.

Well, I was *always* worried about him, but ever since we'd picked up that pilot a week ago, it'd gotten worse.

Flint was naïve, and too friendly for his own good. He gave away too much of himself too easily, and when he was a kid, there were countless times I'd had to rescue him from the schemes of less well-meaning boys.

But the stakes were much higher now.

That's why I had to convince him to stop looking after Jayden and let Doc Aspen handle it.

"Hey, sis," he said, coming up behind me.

I turned. "Hey."

"Find anything new this morning?" he asked as we joined a queue.

"Yeah," I said. "A different species of callia vine. I caught a navic in flower too. I'm hoping the petals will help with bruising."

Flint grinned. "Maybe I can try them out on Jayden."

My expression darkened, and a hard lump formed in my chest. "I want you to stop treating him, Flint."

"What?" he said as we shuffled forward. "We can't just stop treating him!"

"No," I said. "I want *you* to stop treating him. Let Doc do it."

Now Flint's expression darkened. "I'm *training* to be a doctor, Nettle. He's my first real patient. Why would you want me to give up this opportunity?"

Feeling uncomfortable, I looked down. "There'll be other opportunities."

"So what if there are?" Flint said. "That's still no reason to give up *this* one. Besides, I like Jayden."

Damn. That was *exactly* what I had been worried about. The discomfort hardened into hatred. "He works for Central. He's a *soldier*, Flint."

"Your point being?"

Flint's eyes flashed something, but so did mine.

"Don't pretend you don't know," I hissed, keeping my voice low. Already a few people had glanced around at us.

We were at the ovens now, and Flint grabbed a flatbread round. "He's a couple years older than us at most, Nettle. He had nothing to do with what happened to Mama and Dad."

I took a round too, and pushed away memories of that day. That horrible day. "They're all the same," I said. "All heartless. You can't trust him, Flint. He's going to take advantage of you, I know it."

Flint had been about to move off, but he stopped in his tracks and turned to face me. "When are you going to stop trying to control everything that happens to me, Nettle?"

He'd said that pretty loud. Lots of people were staring at us. Cheeks flaming, I grabbed his arm and moved us towards the fruits, smoked meats, and salads, saying nothing.

"Nettle?"

This wasn't going to plan. Flint had always been easy-going, and happy to let me take care of him, so what was behind this change? Loneliness? Resentment?

Why?

He'd adored me when we were young. I'd cuddled him at night when he was scared, told him stories when he was sad, and held his hand as we'd trekked through the forest. It was *me* who'd pulled him to his feet whenever he'd stumbled. *Me* who'd turned survival into a game. *Me* who'd defended him when the older boys mocked his tears. I'd been his rock...

But he'd also been mine. My coping mechanism. Still was, in many ways.

My insides cramped up, utter helplessness threatening to crush me.

He didn't need me anymore, and I might lose him.

That possibility terrified me far more than any friendship that might develop between him and Jayden. I'd promised... I'd promised...

My throat closed over. "I just don't want anything to happen to you, Flint," I said at last. "I don't know what I'd do if..."

Flint exhaled. "I know," he said, "but I'm not five years old anymore, Nettle."

We loaded up our flatbreads in silence, then took seats in the cool shade of a palm-thatched pavilion.

As we chewed in awkward silence, I looked out over the lush valley, our home for the past fifteen years. We'd accomplished so much in that time—food security, medicines, sanitation. A life better than the one we'd left behind. A life where Flint and I could be safe. A life I couldn't let anyone threaten.

Especially not some stupid pilot from Central.

"Flint?"

"Yeah?"

"Sorry. I overstepped," I said. "But let me watch your back, ok? Especially when he heals up a bit. You let me be me. I'll let you be you. Deal?"

Flint grinned. "Deal," he said. "But seriously, Nettle, this *is* an opportunity. Not just for me, but for all of us. When he finds out the truth..."

My sceptical eyes met his eager ones. "Don't get your hopes up, Flint," I said. "He's not like us."

Chapter 5

Jayden

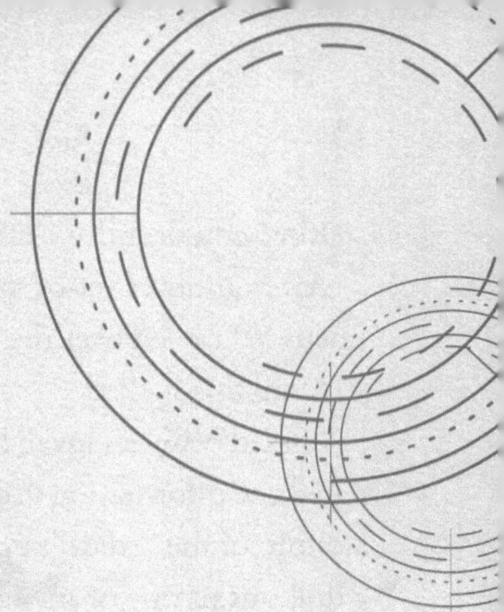

THREE WEEKS HAD PASSED. I lay on my bed, frustrated, bored, and uncomfortable, doing the physio exercises Flint had assigned me. The crash had messed me up pretty bad. It would take ages to heal fully. Right now, I couldn't even walk on my own. In the pause between sets, I looked out the entrance, dazzlingly bright and beckoning in its promise of freedom—and hence mocking. An insurmountable green wall I was trapped behind.

I slammed my head back down on the pillow. There would be no rescue. I knew that. I would be presumed dead. Maybe it would be better if I *was* dead. Instead, I didn't know *what* I was.

At first, I'd assumed I was a hostage, but that word hadn't been mentioned since that conversation I wasn't supposed to hear. *No* plans had been mentioned, in fact, so I didn't know what the rebels planned to do with me, or why they were rehabilitating me. The only thing I was fairly sure of was that they had no intention of returning me.

But I *would* get back. Even if I had to hike every stinking mile.

I needed to get my parents and sister out of 'Wormsville'—not its real name, but what everyone called the warren of underground billets we were consigned to.

Did they still hold out hope? Or were they so exhausted earning their miserable wages processing oscillium, starved of sunlight and treated like the dirt they lived beneath, that they didn't have any energy left even to worry about me?

Deep down I knew neither was true. They'd be crying. Just like we'd all cried over Katie.

But I couldn't think about that now. I just had to recover.

After another set of knee bends, ankle flexes, and arm raises, I manoeuvred myself over the bedpan.

Man, this sucked.

I hated being an invalid. I hated having nothing to do or watch. And I hated the information vacuum I was in. My family at least could look at a photo of me. I didn't even have that—just memories of making Sarah a doll out of one of my old shirts, sneaking her extra food or medicine, and giving her my leisure passes so she could breathe real air.

But Flint would be here soon. He tended me daily, and Nettle hovered close by too—presumably to make sure I didn't do anything to her brother as my strength returned.

I didn't. What purpose would it serve? If I was to escape this place, I needed to be fully recovered—and trusted.

So I put on a smile, thanked him. Joked sometimes. Even pretended to like all the weird things they fed me.

Nettle continued to glower, but even though she scared the hell out of me, I chose to smile at her too.

It was pretty easy considering the view. She was stunning—when I ignored the fact she'd happily slit my throat. Her dark hair and golden-brown skin were both smooth, and her stormy eyes with their perfectly arched brows sat wide above high cheekbones. I could tell she was lean and muscular beneath the loose fatigues she always wore, and she carried herself with strength and a certain amount of rigidity. That kind of complemented the fact that her neutral expression was a scowl.

Flint shared her looks, but his face wore a perpetual grin, and here it came now, right on cue, with the thundercloud of Nettle trailing behind.

I pasted on my best smile. "Hey, Flint." I'd learnt early on that greeting Nettle was not a good idea.

"Hey, Jayden," he replied. "How are those exercises going?"

"Fine," I said. "Getting easier."

After removing the bedpan, Flint helped me to a sitting position, gave me a shave, then checked me over. "I think you're ready for something more challenging. How about we take a walk outside?"

I blinked in surprise. "Seriously?"

"Yeah," he said. "But don't worry, we won't go too far."

I looked with longing at the outside world, wishing I could go miles. "Let's do it."

First, Flint pulled the screen and got me into some new fatigues—surprisingly light and breathable—then helped me down from the bed. As we were about the same height and build, broad in the shoulder and narrow in the hip, his support worked well as I took my first tentative steps.

Nettle followed us of course. Maybe she thought that because I could stagger now, I might knife Flint in the back or something.

We paused at the entrance so I could rest and let my eyes adjust. I looked up, down, around. The rebel base was set inside a cave complex on the south side of a vast valley. It sheltered native subtropical orchards that were more like tidy forests, as well as lush terraces planted with indigenous vegetables and herbs. Animals grazed throughout, watchful rebels and their children tending them. A waterfall on the upper ridge fed a substantial lake that drained between two hills, and a few composite clay domes dotted the clearer areas.

It looked idyllic, if primitive. So different from the metal structures and enormous faceted glass domes of the colony, with its factories and towering chimneys.

It also didn't look like a rebel base.

"You weren't kidding when you said this was mostly a farm," I said to Flint as we made our way down.

"Why would I kid about that?"

"I don't know."

"Well, yeah, it's like I told you, we've just constructed what we need to live. That's all we're trying to do."

I furrowed my brow. "That's it?"

"Yep."

"But you could do that in the colony."

Flint was silent and seemed far away.

"What?"

"I suppose it's time to tell you."

"Tell me what?"

Flint sighed. "*No one* will be able to live in the colony for much longer," he said. "Osivirius isn't compatible with Earth tech. More and more dead-zones keep developing. In another fifty years, the entire planet might be a giant dead-zone. Anything electronic will become useless, and there'll be no way of sustaining the current systems. Some people might be able to leave before that happens, but everyone else will need to learn to live simply, in harmony with this place, or they won't be able to live at all."

"That can't be true," I scoffed, given the rebels were *behind* the dead-zones. "Why would Central lie about that? And why would they care about a few people going off and living in caves?" Had Flint been brainwashed? Or was he trying to pull one over on me? Probably the rebels' real headquarters was somewhere else, and this was just part of their logistics chain.

From behind, Nettle huffed. "Because Central is *causing* the dead-zone expansion. Something gets triggered every time oscillium gets ripped out of the ground, and the colony commander doesn't want to face up to that fact. It'll hurt the bottom line, and credits are all that matter to him," she spat. "He can't stand us living out here because he can't control us and bleed us dry with the rising cost of resources." Flint had stopped moving, so I twisted to look at her. There was so much anger in her expression. So much passion. "He hates us because we don't need him."

Flint shrugged. "Here, we are free; we are *something*. In the colony, people are just resources. Things to be used."

I stayed silent as we hobbled forward a few more steps. Though I hated to admit it, he was right. Especially those of us in Wormsville. That's why I was determined to get my family out of there—once I got out of *here*.

My mind flew back to the subway station, where I'd taken the stairs and they'd taken the train into that endless, black tunnel. Man, they'd be struggling right now with my credits no longer coming in. Worse, they'd be doing it while thinking I'd gotten myself killed on this mission.

My parents hadn't liked it when I'd put up my hand. They'd tried to talk me out of it, but I'd blown off their fears, ignored Sarah's protests, told them I'd be fine. Did Sarah hate me now? Did she curl up, exhausted, on her bunk in our little underground box and glare at my picture? Or did she cry at night, her insides hollow with regret like mine?

Dammit! I hadn't meant to put them through this torture for a second time, I'd just wanted to give us a better life!

Screw these rebels and their crazy ideas. If it weren't for them, I'd be home now, slowly digging us out of that suffocating pit.

But all I could do was play along.

We reached a garden terrace, and Flint eased me down onto a seat. He and Nettle began picking various herbs. After the weeks cooped up in my room, the sun felt good on my face, and the scent of the flowers and herbs was like nothing I'd ever experienced before—except whenever Nettle walked by. I still found it strange that she smelt so good.

With nothing better to do, I sat quietly scanning the terrain, getting my bearings, looking for the easiest route out.

"Hey, Nettle," Flint said. "Go pick some of yourself, I'm running low."

She laughed. It was the first time I'd ever heard her do so. I'd honestly thought her incapable of it. I turned towards her.

"You scared of being stung again?" she joked.

Flint grinned. "Maybe."

Nettle rolled her eyes. "Fine."

I couldn't take my eyes off her. She looked so relaxed in that moment. It was a side of her I'd never seen. Her dark hair riffled in the breeze and her liquid brown eyes became almost playful. Suddenly, I wished she'd look at me.

No. What was I thinking? The last thing I needed in my life was *that* kind of complication. She probably still wanted to kill me!

Besides, I couldn't afford to get attached to *anyone*. As soon as I could work out a way to get out of this valley, I was leaving this tech black hole and calling for an evac. I'd claim the reward and get my family out of the oscillium plant and into a biodome instead. We'd move out of our tin can in Wormsville to a three-bedroom apartment in one of the crystal towers and...

"What are you staring at?"

Nettle's voice was cold and hard as usual. Refocusing, I realised I'd still been looking in her direction. "Nothing," I said.

"Oh, so I'm nothing now. Typical."

"I didn't mean that—" I began.

"She really suits her name, doesn't she?" Flint laughed. "I chose well."

Still flustered, I blurted, "Yeah, I mean, no, I mean— Wait, *you* chose it?"

Grinning, Flint held out his forearm for me to brace against, only offering as much assistance as I needed to get up out of my seat.

"We picked new ones when we got here. Natural things," he said as he took my weight for the journey back to the caves. "My sister's a bit prickly, so... Nettle it was."

"I suppose 'cactus' wouldn't really have worked," I quipped.

Flint laughed. "Yeah, and she wasn't pretty enough for 'rose'," he joked.

My gaze unconsciously found her. "Maybe not then..." I said before thinking about it. Nettle narrowed her eyes at me, and, embarrassed, I cleared my throat. "Uh, what about 'flint'?" I asked.

"You don't wanna know," he said.

"He nearly burnt the camp down," Nettle explained from over her shoulder as she sauntered ahead with the basket of herbs. "Would have, too, if it wasn't for me." There was something in her voice, a lingering fear.

It made me think of Sarah. And the fire that broke out in the communal kitchen that time. We'd been ten seconds from disaster...

Beside me, Flint groaned. "It was an accident!" he protested. "Kind of funny in hindsight, though."

"It wasn't funny at all," Nettle disagreed. "It was terrifying."

"And you won't let me forget it."

I was about to chime in with something supportive when a black shadow swooped overhead. Instinctively, I pulled Flint down and reached for the sidearm I didn't have. The great, black creature shot over the top of us and landed on a ledge in front of a large cave.

I stared open-mouthed as dozens more of the winged felines—for that's what they were, as far as I could tell—soared in and landed. Subtly leopard patterned or jet black with a lighter underside, they flared powerful wings and back beat a few times before elegantly touching down on their rear paws. Some clutched prey, while another pair carried a great net strung between them via harnesses. It held a huge quantity of what looked like fruit.

That's when I noticed the rebels dismounting.

Once unburdened of their riders, the great cats padded gracefully to one side, where they received the attentions of the puny humans they dwarfed. One yawned, settled its wings, and licked a forepaw, then began rubbing it over a tufted ear. That paw alone was the size of a person's head.

As I continued to gape, something stirred inside me. Not fear exactly, but something a bit like it. I couldn't tear my eyes away from the creatures. Their wingspan was enormous, their fur glossy, and their sabres frightening. They looked like something out of legend. Overhead, more wheeled and soared in a great aerial ballet.

"Beautiful, aren't they?" Flint said. "The Masu."

"Yeah..." I breathed, then finally ripped my eyes away. "They're your transport?"

Nettle huffed. "Transport. Everything is just a 'thing' to you, isn't it? A tool. A means."

Flint shifted his weight to take mine properly again. "Masu are our partners. They're incredibly intelligent," he said. "And yes, they get us around. How do you think we found you so fast and got you back here?"

I looked at the net with its burden of fruit being lowered expertly to the ground, glad I was unconscious for that trip. I might be used to flying, but not like *that*. I preferred to be at the controls. Wait...

"Why have I never seen them before?"

Nettle snorted. "As Flint said, they're not stupid."

I sensed the bite in her words but gazed back up at the great flying cats as we hobbled past, the seed of an idea sprouting.

"How'd you tame them?"

Nettle gave a long-suffering sigh, and Flint looked at me and shook his head. "We didn't."

I screwed up my face. "Then how—"

"They tamed *us*."

Now I was even more confused.

Flint got an almost dreamy look on his face. "They have a calming presence, and mind-link with us. We don't share words so much as... impressions, desires, understandings. It's hard to explain. You just have to experience it."

I drew my brows together. "And how do I do that?"

Flint grinned. "A bit of Vine's mushroom juice'll do the trick."

That was it? And he seemed to be offering it to me. Why? It made no sense, but hey, I'd take it.

When I looked at Flint's enormous grin though, the tiniest bit of shame stabbed. In any other circumstances, he and I could have been friends.

I broke eye contact and swung my gaze back to the Masu. Many of them now sat regally, like great sphinxes, while the rebels stroked their necks and laughed, eyes shining. The longing planted by that seed of an idea rose inside me.

What would it be like to fly on one?

And how much faster could I get out of here if I did...

Even when I regained my strength, escape via trekking was unlikely to succeed, much as I'd tried to convince myself otherwise, and now that I knew the rebels had these things, I'd probably be caught even faster.

These Masu were my only real ticket out of here, but what would it take to learn to ride one of them? How much more embroiled in the rebels' lives would I have to get? Already, I felt a twinge of guilt about lying to Flint; using his good-naturedness against him.

But I had to get back. With my credits no longer coming in, my family would've had to stop saving, which would doom them to life underground. And I didn't work my butt off to become a pilot just for that to happen. I wouldn't let them die as expendable nobodies. Not again.

"I want to try it," I said.

Nettle turned to me, head cocked, brows drawn. "Riding Masu is nothing like flying a 'thopter," she said. There was surprise in her voice, and though her expression was still serious, her bristliness had disappeared.

I blinked, astonished that she'd just spoken to me.

In a non-threatening way.

For once.

Even sounding... impressed.

I lowered my eyes. For some reason, her positive regard scared me more than her hostility...

And deepened the sense of guilt I was desperately trying to squash.

But if they were keeping me in the dark, I'd sure as hell keep them in the dark too.

Still, I swallowed. Locked eyes. "I want to try it," I repeated.

Flint adjusted his grip. "Better exercise hard then," he said with his customary grin. "You'll need everything you've got just to hang on."

Chapter 6
Nettle

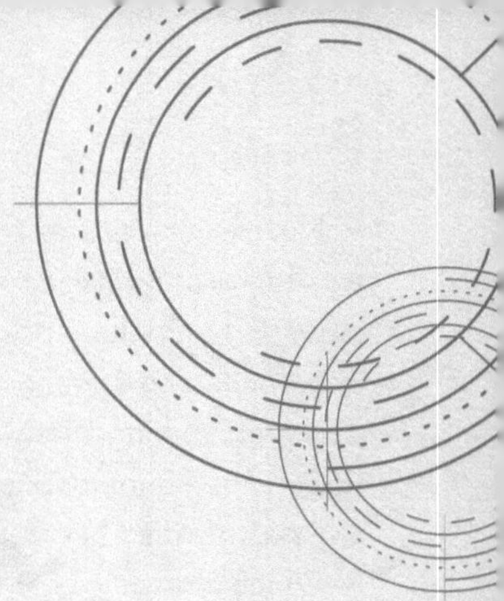

CHAPERONING FLINT AND JAYDEN was taking a toll on my research. It was six weeks since he'd crashed, and that stupid pilot insisted on being exercised twice a day now. Flint thought it was marvellous, but it essentially confined me to base. No foraging trips on Timu for me. Frustrated and edgy, I rested my head against the Masu's silky shoulder as we both lay in the shade, waiting for the cooler evening to descend.

Timu put an image of us flying together in my mind, and longing assaulted me anew.

I miss it too, I communicated. *But I have to keep an eye on Flint.*

Timu created an image of Flint, Jayden and me, then erased my figure.

Anxiety replaced the longing. *No*, I said, *I won't leave him and Flint alone. I don't trust Jayden.*

Timu rumbled understanding, but formed an image of cubs growing up.

I sucked in a breath. *It's not the same*, I said. *Flint's my brother.*

Timu rumbled in a sceptical way, and this time constructed a tonal image of three interconnected rings of light that thrummed with life, never staying still. The Balance. My head always hurt whenever he showed me this, because it reminded me of diagrams I'd seen of electrons orbiting a nucleus, except this was dynamic and fractal and overwhelming. Simultaneously microscopic and vast; in the web, but outside it too; endless loops of sound and light that knit the universe together, and yet its own contained entity. Music made into matter.

And it was not inert.

No, passion radiated from it, an agonised joy. Sorrow and delight in equal measure, all wrapped up in a profound and powerful peace. A sense that everything belonged. To the Masu, the Balance allowed the cycles of life and death to nurture and renew every interconnected thing. The great cats understood this implicitly, and Timu had shown this image to me countless times as I was growing up beside him—to comfort and reassure me whenever the grief got too much.

Which it usually did, in a terrifying sort of way.

But not this time.

I knew what Timu was trying to get at, and I didn't agree.

Leave the Balance out of this. Jayden did not end up here for my benefit. Or anyone else's benefit. It was completely random.

Timu merely sustained the image, placing a memory of our first contact within the whirling embrace of musical light.

I sat up, annoyed. *It's not the same,* I insisted, and looked into his soft, green eyes. *The rest of the colonists aren't like us.*

Turning away from Timu, I considered the lowering sun, vibrant pink and orange staining the sky around it. *Flint'll be going to get Jayden for supper*, I said. *Time for me to go.*

Seemingly indifferent, Timu yawned and fluffed his wings, ready to settle for the evening, but he did give me an encouraging nose-bump as I rose. I hoped he was right, and everything *would* be fine. But I wasn't ready to believe that yet, even if the signals coming from Jayden weren't as dangerous as I expected.

To be honest, he confused me.

I had been expecting him to be difficult, mocking, aggressive. I thought I might catch him with a cunning look in his eye, or trying to trick information out of Flint. But Jayden didn't complain and seemed grateful for all Flint did for him. He sounded genuinely impressed by all we'd accomplished here and talked about wanting to stop being a burden as soon as possible.

Still, I hurried to the hospital cave. When I got there, Flint was handing Jayden a trekking pole. "Reckon you're ready for it?" he asked.

"I guess we'll find out," Jayden said, tamping it against the floor a few times and testing his weight. He looked up. "Hey, Nettle. Fancy seeing you here."

Under Flint's tutelage, he'd gotten more comfortable with me over the past few weeks, but I still scowled.

Flint laughed.

"Join us for supper?" Jayden asked.

"I don't think we have a choice, Jayden," Flint said with a wink.

I scowled again and crossed my arms. "That's right. You don't."

Jayden swung a leg forward and planted the pole, then moved the other leg. Turning to Flint, he grinned. It was the same eager smile he got whenever Masu flew overhead. So big his teeth showed.

"This'll work," he said, and swung-thumped again. His bicep and forearm strained as he put his weight on the pole, as did the muscles around his neck. Despite myself, I admitted to a small amount of admiration for his efforts.

Soon enough, he was drawing abreast with me, so I swivelled and walked ahead. Best not to look at him right now.

"Don't you wish you had a sister as protective as Nettle, Jayden?" Flint said from behind.

"Works the other way around for me and my sister," Jayden replied as he swung-thumped a few more paces. "I'm the protective one."

His voice dropped a little as he said this, and I couldn't help myself. I looked over my shoulder, curious.

"Did something happen to her?" I asked.

Jayden let out a heavy breath before answering. "She nearly died. My other sister *did* die."

I stopped in my tracks. With Flint, I looked at Jayden.

"What happened?" asked Flint.

Jayden took a few seconds to answer. Worked his jaw a bit. "A virus ripped through the colony. I was twelve, and got it mild. Sarah was ten, and... got it real bad. So did little Katie."

"The medical staff didn't stop it? Help?" Flint asked, aghast.

Jayden scowled. "For those who lived aboveground, yes, but not in the underground billets. When my parents recovered enough, they tried to get help, but us lowly worms weren't 'valuable' enough to treat. A bunch of people died. Including Katie."

My own memories stirred. "Bastards," I grunted.

Jayden looked at me, and I met his eyes for a long moment. There was an understanding there; a passion. I turned away.

"Bastards alright," Jayden agreed. He swung-thumped another pace. "That's why I worked my butt off to become a pilot," he said. "So I could earn enough to get us aboveground. I was never gonna let that happen again."

His swing-thumps became more aggressive, and our pace picked up.

"Did you do it?" asked Flint. "Did you get aboveground?"

Jayden clenched his teeth. "Not yet."

Flint and I exchanged a look. He made a 'well that was unexpected' face, then grabbed Jayden's elbow as his pole slipped. "Whoa, not so fast!" he said, and steadied Jayden as he wobbled a bit.

"Sorry," said Jayden. "Thinking about that always gets me riled up."

"With good reason," said Flint, "but let's not undo all my good work, ok?"

He flashed Jayden a smile, and Jayden returned it, though his eyes were still haunted. "Sure," Jayden said. "No one wants that."

"Ready?" Flint asked.

Jayden's answer was a swing-thump.

I stayed where I was, rooted to the spot by a strange uncertainty. Jayden's whole life was centred around caring for his sister, just like mine was around making sure Flint was safe. And he was really determined. I couldn't help admiring that as I let the two of them draw ahead of me.

Stranger still, it seemed he wasn't Central's lapdog after all. He despised them as much as I did.

Remembering my own brush with Central's cruelty, I shook myself, hardening the place that had softened. He was *still* playing their game. Being part of the system. Part of the problem.

I bit my lip. Was that because he hadn't known any better?

Flint looked over his shoulder. "Hey, Nettle. You coming or what?"

"Yeah," I called, uncomfortable. "Just thought I saw something, that's all."

Conflicting thoughts competed in my head as I got moving again, and as I followed the two of them down the gentle slope, watching Jayden's back, I saw again those eyes that for a moment had met mine with such shared intensity...

He had a sister who he loved, just like I loved Flint.

I shook myself.

Didn't matter. He was still a jerk. And dangerous.

But as the warm glow of the firepits came into view, and the aroma of roast palyx invited me in, I revisited the one thought I kept stumbling over.

He hated Central.

I had *not* expected to hear him say that.

Could Flint be right and I be wrong? I wasn't ready to make that call, but as I heard their laughter up ahead, I decided that Flint was probably safe enough here in the valley, and that getting away with Timu would be good for me.

Chapter 7

Jayden

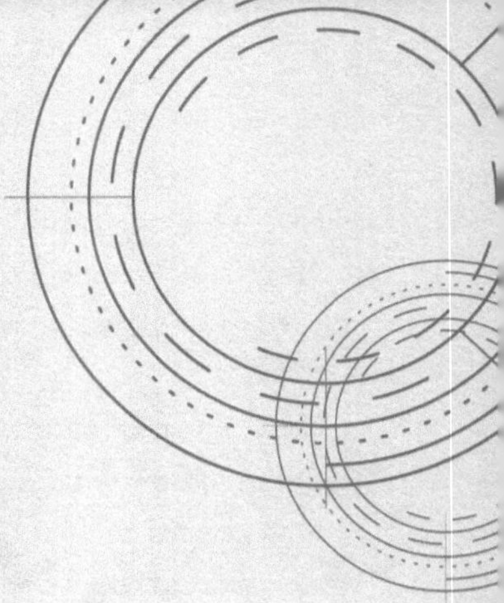

"**H**ey, Jayden, thanks for helping out. We'll make a builder out of you yet." Clay, the site foreman clapped me on the shoulder, and I shot him a grin.

"No worries," I said. "It was fun."

I actually meant it.

I mean, it was hard work—tiring—but seeing the first stage of the block-work dome come together was more satisfying than I thought it would be. I'd been doing things like this for a few months now, beginning in the gardens. The work had served a threefold purpose: recovering my strength, gathering intel, and gaining trust. All directed towards my singular goal of being invited to join a Masu flight.

Some of the awesome creatures coasted overhead now after a successful hunting trip, a horned palyx clasped by one, a slope-backed brinel by another. It wasn't hard to imagine myself riding amongst the group, soaring, banking, flaring to land. The watch changeover would happen soon too, one sentry winging down while another winged up to the ridgeline. That's what I was ultimately aiming for, and every time I saw it, the idea of gliding across that boundary and just not stopping became more and more real. I still missed my family like crazy, but they seemed less far away now.

Stretching aching arms, I waved to Clay and the building crew, intending to have a nice, long soak in the hot springs before supper, but before I'd made it very far along the path back to the caves, I met Doc coming the other way.

"Here to check out the new building?" I asked. "First stage is complete. It's looking good."

"Excellent," replied Doc. "I *did* want to check the progress, but I also wanted to see how *you* were coming along."

"Me?"

"Yes," he said. "I know this must be difficult for you."

I didn't know what to say, so I just shrugged. "Yeah."

Doc clasped my upper arm. "Still, I want you to feel at home here while we decide how to proceed."

I just looked at him. "You intending to let me in on that sometime?"

Doc sighed. "There are many things to consider, and much debate ongoing amongst the leadership team, Jayden, but—yes, eventually."

It seemed that was the best I was going to get. But it didn't matter. I had my own plans.

"Ok," I said. "See you at supper then."

"I'll be serving tonight," he said. "With Lily."

Everyone here took a turn at watch, serving and cleaning about once a month—even Doc and his wife Lily, though they essentially ran this place. The rebels did a lot of things differently. The reason I'd been able to work with the building crew so easily, was that I'd joined the ranks of the kids who were engaged in a kind of 'round robin' after their couple of hours of morning school. They'd rotate through trades or professions until they found something they wanted to pursue in depth, but I simply figured if I learnt as much about the rebels as I could—since they were obviously in no hurry to be rid of me—Central would pay me even more handsomely.

"Enjoy."

I made a move to go, but Doc Aspen clasped my arm again. "Don't think I don't care, Jayden," he said, "but I have a lot of people to look after."

I nodded, not trusting myself to do anything else. His 'care' for the rebels was preventing me from caring for my sister and parents, but I didn't think pointing that out would make any difference right now—and I preferred him to think me compliant.

But… Sarah. Who would keep the creeps away from her now?

I clenched my teeth. "Yeah."

I'm sure Doc noticed the bitter edge in my voice as we parted ways, but given our conversation, it was to be expected. I continued up the path, passing one of the orchards and the mill. Several people waved at me or called greetings, and, getting back into character again, I smiled and waved back. Most of them had regarded me with suspicion at first, but a bit of curiosity had them showing me the ropes soon enough.

My casual investigations had ascertained that about a thousand rebels lived here, with approximately half of them kids, and they had all mastered or were mastering different archaic skills—weaving, carpentry, ceramics, archery. Even the scientists and engineers. There was a small smithy—with my scavenged 'thopter parts piled in a shed beside it—and vast storehouses of dried fruit, meat, and fermented vegetables. I passed one now.

Continuing up the path, I watched another flight of Masu return. Hundreds of them lived in the valley, and they were the rebels' only real means of defence as far as I could tell. The animals could both sense and produce electromagnetic fields. Flint said they had 'stealth fur' as well, that somehow scattered signals. They were like electromagnetic chameleons. Their presence might've had something to do with activating or maintaining the EM wall as well, perhaps simply through sheer numbers, since they congregated in the dead-zones.

Everyone I spoke to was adamant these areas were a natural phenomenon triggered by some kind of destructive resonance amplification. There *had* been a few noted during the original survey of the planet, but according to the rebels, the multiplication had begun when we set up shop here, and was made worse with each new mining operation or other installation. I didn't buy it, but they all sure had their story straight.

As I climbed further, I came to the garden terraces, where teams of rebels toiled in the subtropical heat. There was no denying they worked hard—perhaps harder than we did in the colony because there were no robots and only very rudimentary machines to help—but as I caught parts of their joking chatter, it struck me that there was a deep satisfaction about it all. I didn't remember anyone looking this happy back in the colony. Certainly not anyone in Wormsville. There, the hours were a continuous, artificially-lit blur: an hour's round trip on a bullet-train subway to a twelve-hour shift at an underground processing plant. Sarah always looked half-dead when she came home. So did my parents. Even so, there never seemed to be enough.

Here, there was abundance.

I wished I could show it to them.

I shook myself. What? Once I returned, we'd have abundance *there* too. Everything we could possibly want. I was playing a role here, that's all. It took my mind off sadder thoughts, like how everyone at home must be sure I was dead by now. No, the horizon still called, and everything I was doing was just another step towards it.

When I reached the herb gardens, Flint was there, plucking some white flowers and putting them in a basket. He seemed in a hurry.

"What are those for?" I asked, figuring they might be a remedy of some sort.

"Nettle," he replied. "She needs them for something or other."

Before Flint could say anything more, a Masu and rider came in to land overhead. "Dammit," he said, "I'm late for shift change." He looked at the basket, then at me. "Hey, would you mind taking these to the lab?"

I balked. "By myself?"

Flint grinned. "What? You afraid Nettle's gonna bite you or something?" He thrust the basket at me. "Sorry! Gotta run!"

Stunned, I stood there as he loped off, the basket of flowers dangling from my hand. Twisting my mouth into a grimace, I gazed down at the offending blooms. *Thanks a lot, Flint.* Still grumbling to myself, and annoyed my soak at the springs would be delayed, I hiked in the opposite direction up to the lab.

It was kind of out-of-the-way a bit, right up the top of the switchback path, and took me about ten minutes to get to. I'd known where it was for ages but had never gone inside. Had no reason to—until now.

I'd also never had to deal with Nettle solo. And despite Flint's joking, she probably *would* bite. Verbally anyway.

The lab was one of the few caves to have had a proper door fitted, which made sense, given the equipment inside, and I hesitated on the threshold.

This is stupid, I berated myself. *It's only a delivery. No big deal. I'll be in, then out.*

Inhaling a breath of courage, I knocked on the door.

No answer.

Perplexed, I turned the handle and opened it.

Empty.

Kind of relieved, I stepped inside, intending to deposit the basket on a bench and then leave, when Nettle walked in from a side room, clipboard in hand. She stopped short when she saw me.

"I... I brought you these," I said, holding up the basket and then cursing myself for how ridiculous that must have sounded, like she was my girlfriend or something, and I was giving her a bunch of flowers.

She didn't seem to notice. "I asked Flint to bring them."

"Yeah, I know. He was running late for watch changeover, and I happened to be walking by."

"Oh," said Nettle, making some marks on her clipboard, then absently flicking a hand. "Put them over there, then."

The bench she indicated was against the far wall, which was covered with drawings of plants. They were intricately detailed and vivid, and I spent several moments admiring them before setting the basket down.

"Didn't know you were so interested in botany," Nettle said from behind me.

I flinched; looked at her over my shoulder. "Never really was before now, but these are incredible."

"Thanks."

It took me a moment to realise what that meant. "You drew them?"

"It's part of the job," she said with a shrug.

I gave a low whistle. "Maybe," I said, "but that doesn't negate the talent involved."

Nettle dipped her eyes. Shrugged again. Shyly?

I felt butterflies tingle their way across the inside of my chest.

Dammit. Not now. Not again. I turned back to the artwork. "I recognise this one from when I worked in the orchard. It's the gupi flower."

"That's right," Nettle said, "and this one's a pai-pai flower."

"I love pai-pai!" I said a little too enthusiastically.

Nettle glanced at me from the corner of her eye, a sneaky smile on her lips, and I coughed to hide my embarrassment. My eyes found a drawing of the flowers I just brought up. "Hey, these are the ones in the basket," I said.

"Not quite," Nettle corrected, "but close. A different variety. See, these ones have purple stamens, but the ones in this drawing are red."

I peered at the drawing, picked up a flower to compare. "Oh, you're right."

Putting the flower back in the basket, I scanned the wall again, only now noticing the scientific names listed at the bottom of each drawing. Callia pernistus, opinia serumae, festulastiptus nettlii... Nettlii? "Is this one named after you?" I asked.

I think she actually blushed. "Yeah. I found that one. It's what we make the pipes from."

"Cool," I said. "I guess that's your favourite then."

"No," she said, pointing to a flower at the far end. "This one's my favourite. The navic."

The bloom she indicated was bright yellow and somewhat trumpet-shaped, but with a snail-like addition where it attached to the stem. Its curves were sensuous, inviting.

"The flower itself is beautiful," Nettle said into the silence, "but it's the mystery of them that intrigues me. I've yet to discover what triggers their blooming. It's not seasonal, and it doesn't seem like there's a regular flowering interval for the individual trees either."

"Random?" I suggested.

Nettle twisted her lips. "No, nothing's ever random."

The whites of her eyes startled suddenly wider, like she'd said something inappropriate, then she looked away rather quickly. Took the cover off a microscope. "I've got work to do."

She pulled a drawer and found a couple of scalpels, then plucked a flower from the basket and laid it on a board, intent.

I hovered there for a moment.

"You can go now," she said without looking at me, back stiff.

The dismissal was obvious, but for a few minutes there, she'd been a different person. Someone clever, and modest, and open. Even a little playful. Certainly pleasant. Maybe I could get that person to come out again.

Dammit. It was stupid, I knew, but I really *wanted* to get that person to come out again.

I took in the curves of the navic flower once more. "Ok," I said, then left.

Chapter 8

Nettle

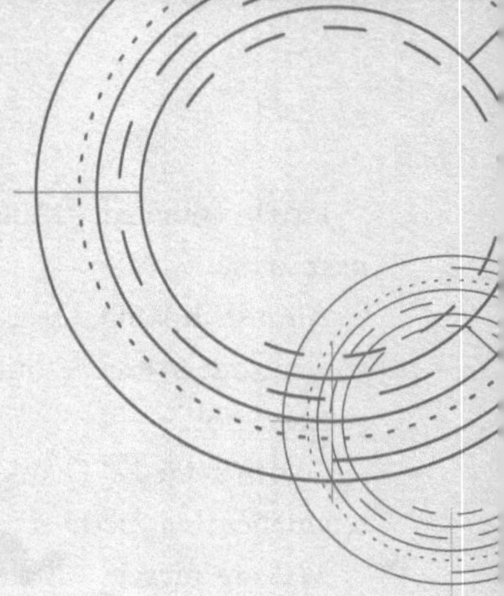

T HE AROMA OF BRINEL stew tantalised me as I made my way from the lab to the firepits. Seasoned with pimmel and atica, it was one of my favourites, and my stomach grumbled in both acknowledgement of that fact and anticipation.

Picking up a gourd bowl from a stack, I joined the shortest queue.

"It's your favourite tonight," Doc said as he emptied the ladle into my bowl.

I smiled. "You remembered."

He smiled too, his eyes crinkling at the corners. "Of course I remember. How could I not?"

From the next pot along, Grandma Lily laughed. "That's right! Especially with me to remind him!"

I snorted, a burst of love for these two warming me as much as the fire. They weren't actually our grandparents—more like a great aunt and uncle once removed—though they'd cared for us as if they were.

"Enjoy, sweetie," Lily said.

With the steaming concoction now in hand, I scanned for Flint, then remembered he was on watch. My heart sank a little. It looked like I'd be dining solo tonight.

There were groups I could've joined, I suppose, but without Flint to lubricate the conversation, I tended to feel awkward just inserting myself. So, looking for a relatively empty log to sit on, I took a chance on someone being brave enough to join me instead.

I was just savouring the first mouthful when a familiar figure blocked the heat of the fire.

Jayden coughed. "Mind if I sit here?" he asked, indicating the spot next to me.

Almost choking, I searched my mind for something, anything, that I could use as an excuse, but came up empty. I swallowed my mouthful. "I suppose not."

Jayden smiled. "Thanks," he said, and lowered himself down a good ten inches to my left.

Making myself a little smaller, I took another spoonful of stew and levered apart the tender meat with my tongue before chewing. I shouldn't have been so forthcoming in the lab. Shouldn't have let his interest in my work lull me into letting my guard down.

But at the same time, it had been nice to have someone compliment my work. Nice to be the expert with a curious student.

Out of the corner of my eye, I saw Jayden take a cautious sip of the liquid.

"Oh, man," he said. "What do they put in here? It's *so* good!" He followed that exclamation with an enormous spoonful.

"Pimmel and atica," I supplied. "My favourites."

"I can see why," Jayden garbled between chews. "Which vegetables?"

I considered my bowl, wondering at myself, but enjoying his enthusiasm, and understanding why Flint liked him so much. "This white one is soba root, and the orange is bago. The green spheres are dib-dib seeds. The pods were dried a few weeks back."

Jayden grinned. "How many of those did you name?"

Heat flushed my cheeks. "Just the dib-dibs," I mumbled. "I was seven."

Jayden cocked his head. "It's a good name. You don't think so?"

I shrugged. "It works, I suppose."

"What about pai-pai, and nac-nac? Those yours too?"

I let out a breath. "Yes, if you must know. I just started calling them that and the names stuck, ok?"

Jayden laughed. "I remember Sarah had funny names for things. Katie too." His face fell. "I miss them."

A little hollow place opened up in my chest, but I didn't want to go down that conversation path.

Still lost in his own memories, Jayden took another big scoop of stew. Chewed it thoughtfully. Tapped his spoon against the bowl.

I cocked my head. "New spoon?"

His expression immediately lifted, and he turned to me, a huge smile lighting up his face. "Yeah, made it myself. Clay showed me how." He held it out for me to admire.

I admit I did. Maybe this crazy idea of Doc's to integrate him would work after all. "That's... actually pretty good."

"Thanks," he said, lowering his eyes in modesty. "It's the first thing I've made since... well, since I made Sarah a doll out of an old shirt." He looked self-conscious.

He'd...? "You made your sister a doll? That's really sweet." The words were out of my mouth before I thought about them. What was going on? Where was my brain?

But I knew that kind of love.

It was the same kind that had given eight-year-old me the idea to make a 'guardian Masu' for Flint out of a lump of clay and some feathers.

And it tugged at me.

"Thanks." Jayden's toothy grin stayed plastered on his face as he kept looking at me. "Wasn't a patch on your artistry though."

I said nothing. Stared. Blinked. "Oh! My drawings!"

He laughed, eyes sparkling. "Yeah, of course your drawings. They're amazing."

"They're technically accurate."

"They're more than technically accurate. They're beautiful. Don't underrate yourself."

His knee nudged mine; a playful gesture, but it caught me off guard, and an unexpected warmth that had nothing to do with the fire flooded me. As he held my gaze, something zipped through my chest, and I felt a strange compulsion to move closer to him, though I stayed completely still. His gleaming smile, the perfect wave in his dark brown hair, and the thick brows above his sparkling eyes all but filled my vision.

The silence stretched to awkwardness, and, getting a hold of myself, I quickly shovelled some stew into my mouth to avoid the need to fill it with words. Jayden followed my lead.

"Thanks," I said after I'd swallowed, and searched for a new topic. "You still working on the dome?"

"Stage one got finished today, so I thought I'd try metalwork now," Jayden said between mouthfuls. "Make myself a knife." He must've seen me flinch, because he added, "For eating."

"Oh, of course. Yeah. Useful." I scooped again, feeling over-warm now, and confused at the way my head and heart wouldn't agree with each other. One kept marvelling at how enjoyable this conversation was, while the other kept wanting to shut it down. "Hope it turns out as well as the spoon."

"We'll see I guess."

"Yeah."

He looked like he wanted to say something else, but without any encouragement from me, it didn't come out till he'd finished his bowl and rested it on his knees. "Hey, Nettle... reckon we can be friends yet?"

I had just scraped the last morsels of stew onto my own spoon and had it halfway to my mouth. It hovered there as I considered the question, scared of what it implied.

"I... maybe. We'll see."

Shoving the spoon in my mouth, I chewed fast and stood. "See you round," I said, then fled as slowly as I could manage.

Chapter 9

Jayden

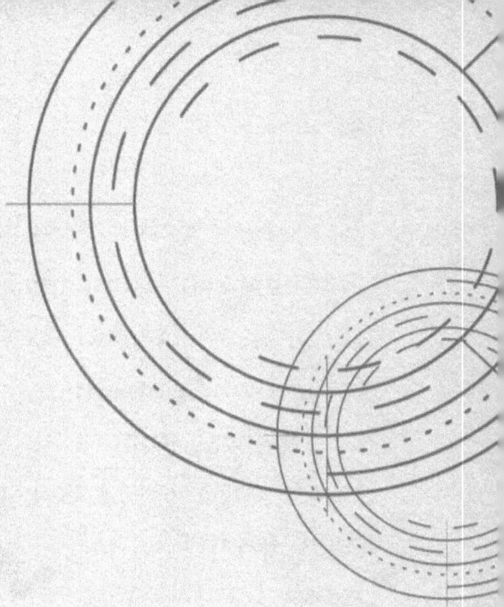

A NOTHER MONTH PASSED. It was just over five now in total, and a glorious morning greeted me, slightly chill now that the dry season had arrived. As I sauntered into the breakfast area, I greeted Nugget, the blacksmith.

"Bah! You abandoned me!" he joked.

"Abandoned?" I raised my hands in mock hurt. "I graduated."

"Ha!" called Flora. "Just like you graduated from the orchard, hey?"

"And the cannery!"

"And the kilns!"

Their ribbing both gratified and disturbed me, though I didn't let that last part show. I guess I had started to feel part of this place, and that felt both right and wrong at the same time.

Oh, I still wanted to get home, and wished I could communicate with my family, tell everyone I was ok, but something had shifted. I'd absolutely *craved* my personal comm-cell when I was lying in the hospital cave recovering. Now I didn't. It freed up so much time not having to deal with the endless alerts, notifications, and messages that always cluttered it, and the lack of 'news' hardly bothered me at all. Stranger still, I found sitting around a fire telling jokes and stories, or seeing the look on Flint's face after I'd won yet another game of checkers against him *way* more satisfying than being on the other side of a screen. I also had more energy than I'd ever had before.

The realisation had crept up on me, but now that I'd noticed it... well, I was still working out what it meant.

Pushing uncertainty aside and taking a seat by Clay, I took the knife

I'd made with Nugget's help and cut open a gupi fruit. The blade wasn't anything fancy, but the sight of its smooth lines made me smile. With the spoon Clay had shown me how to carve, I scooped out the fruit's innards and popped each spoonful into my mouth, savouring the taste.

This was something I'd definitely miss. We ate mostly synth food in the colony. The real stuff grown in the biodomes was saved for the high-ups in Central. They got their beef and roast potatoes, and we got mush, but when I told the agriculture department about the vast range of edible things Osivirius had to offer—which I'd learnt about primarily from Nettle—that would be another thing in our fortunes to change.

As the conversation went on around me, I imagined training teams to identify and gather saplings and seeds. We'd set up efficient farms. Fields and orchards all cultivated in neat rows. Satellite colonies could be established, and maybe I'd be in charge of—

"Hey Jayden, wanna come hunting?"

I nearly choked as Flint slammed his hand down on my shoulder in greeting, but a grin soon split my face. "Serious?"

"Totally. I just cleared it with Doc. He thinks you're ready."

My grin widened. "You bet," I said.

It was the moment I'd been waiting for. My ticket home.

"Ok!" Flint's grin was equally wide. "Let's get you a mushroom juice chaser!"

There was a fungus here—miyu—that made mind-linking with the Masu safer, easier, and more mutual. With it, Masu and rider could act as a single unit. I couldn't wait.

"Tank me up!"

As we passed the sleeping area, I ducked in to grab the bow I'd also made a few months back, and followed Flint to the enormous den, where many of the Masu slept. The miyu infusion was made there too, in a small side-cave. The Masu themselves ate the mushrooms whole, but that could kill a human, so we would consume a diluted concoction. Nettle was already waiting in front of the brew room when we arrived, but the odour of the miyu drowned out her subtle fragrance.

I smiled at her—genuinely.

My fear was gone now, firmly replaced by respect and... maybe something more. I found myself noticing when she wasn't around, anyway, and kind of wishing she was.

Well, maybe more than kind of.

Sometimes I even found excuses to visit her in the lab.

Ok, I regularly manufactured excuses.

And though no easy rapport had developed—not by a long shot—her walls *had* come down, and she at least seemed to tolerate me.

"You coming too?" I asked.

"My brother might trust you," she said, "but I don't."

Even though it was a fair call, her words still stung. More than they should. "Whatever," I said.

Huh. What did I care? I was outta here. Back to a hero's welcome, just as soon as the opportunity presented itself.

Flint cleared his throat. "Now," he said, "when you drink this, it's gonna feel weird."

My illusory homecoming reel stopped abruptly, and a twinge of uneasiness wriggled through my stomach. I compressed my lips into a thin line. "What kind of weird?"

"Spacey for a bit, like you're falling," he said. "That's when the Masu will open a mind-link, and you've gotta trust it'll catch you. Accept it."

The wriggling got worse. "What happens if I don't?"

The corner of Nettle's mouth lifted in a smirk. "Same as the effects of standing unshielded at the epicentre of a titanic EMP—neuropsychiatric disorders. That's what happened to Vine."

The whip-thin Vine brewed the miyu mushroom infusion, and had a tic in his neck. He grinned kind of stupidly most of the time, and tried to catch butterflies that weren't there. I'd noticed a few other rebels who seemed a bit whacked in the head too. The sick feeling in my stomach amplified as he gave me a salute.

"Don't worry, you'll be fine," said Flint, pulling at me. "Hasn't happened since first contact. We didn't have miyu then, and had no idea what we were doing. Neither did the Masu. It was kinda scary. Us kids were ok, but the control-freaks really couldn't handle it. The Masu are much better at making connections now, especially with the miyu to help. So just go with it." He held out a wooden shot-glass to me. "Ready?"

For the first time, this plan didn't seem so watertight. For whatever reason, I thought *I'd* be in charge of the mind-link, not the Masu. Now, not only would I have to trust myself to this creature and risk breaking my mind, I might blow my cover in the process. What if I couldn't conceal my true motives? What would happen if the rebels found out I'd been deceiving them?

Bracing myself, I nodded and took the cup from Flint's hand, then followed them into the den proper. Once we were inside the massive open cavern, three enormous Masu padded towards us. I'd never been this close to them before, and it occurred to me that any one of them could kill me as easily as look at me. Nettle and Flint headed straight for two of them, embracing the great beasts and stroking the fur of their chests. Flint's head perhaps reached the Masu's chin. I swallowed.

The third Masu cocked its head at me, as if assessing whether or not I was a worthy rider, and those worms that had been wriggling around in my stomach solidified into a lead ball. What if it didn't accept *me*? What if it saw right through me, laid bare my plans, and refused to catch me? Would my brain be screwed anyway? Or would it just latch onto my jugular? I felt my breaths come short and sharp so I held them... then blew out a breath. Grit my teeth.

I was in this now. I couldn't back out. I had no other means of escape.

Flint beckoned me over. "This is Shana. She's gentle and very experienced with first-bonds. Say 'hi' to her."

I gave a nervous smile. "Hi," I said, half-raising my hand.

Nettle rolled her eyes. "Touch her, you dolt."

I shot her an irritated glance and blew out another breath. I would *not* let her see my fear. But as I turned back to Shana, my mind sent out a desperate plea: *Don't screw up my brain. Don't screw up my brain. And don't kill me. Please don't kill me.* Taking a pace forward, I placed my hand on Shana's chest, and shouted in alarm as her huge forepaw swung around and hugged my shoulder.

Nettle cackled.

Flint refrained from laughing, but he couldn't quite suppress a smirk. "Ok, this is good. Time to drink."

He and Nettle tossed their infusions down their throats, and, after a final gulp, I followed a moment later. The brew was bitter, and burned as I forced it down my throat. At first, that was all I felt, but then I seemed to expand and... tip. I couldn't feel the ground beneath my feet. Didn't know whether I was up, down, or sideways. I felt a lurch in my stomach, like what happens in turbulence, or free-fall. I wanted to scream, to grip onto something solid, but there was nothing. My brain was going to be screwed for sure.

I fought; resisted; then fell.

And fell.

And fell.

A 'presence' caught me. Anchored me. Shana. I sensed the name rather than heard it, and I sensed her say 'Jayden' like she was vibrating the strings of my very essence and making the world's fabric sing it with her. Safety accompanied the sensation, and something like... humour. Was a *cat* going to laugh at me too?

But I was so relieved, I just sank into the feeling, accepted the connection... and somehow understood it was genuinely two-way. I could break it now if I wanted, and would be just fine.

But I didn't want to. And couldn't understand why anyone *would* want to, for I felt embraced by rings of light and sound that somehow went around me and through me, but were also part of me. They held me in a cradle of peace. A sense that I belonged. That everything belonged.

A moment later, unbounded ecstasy exploded within me, and my senses amplified a hundredfold. Not only could I feel the ground beneath my feet, but I could feel every tiny bump in it. Colours became vivid, and sounds distinct. The air seemed electrified, humming with subliminal music, and I was somehow part of it, sitting on the windowsill between human and divine.

Feeling like some kind of superhero, I let the amazingness burst from my mouth as a joyous whoop.

Awesome, you made it.

Flint's mouth hadn't moved. My superhuman expansion shrank in on itself.

Don't freak out. The Masu facilitate intercommunication. It's how they make coordinated flight manoeuvres and attacks.

O..k... Uncertain, I tested out the link, then saw Nettle watching me with laughter in her eyes... and a really pretty smile.

My stomach flip-flopped.

Uh, are my thoughts private? I asked Flint.

More or less, he answered. *You have to deliberately reach out. Somehow the Masu know when we want to talk. I've only ever heard Nettle call me an idiot when she wants me to hear it.*

I risked a glance at Nettle, but she seemed occupied with her Masu and betrayed no reaction to her brother's remark.

Then she looked right at me.

Time to saddle-up, fly-boy. Nettle's mind-voice held a note of mockery but also... surprise? Challenge? It kind of reminded me of the way my pilot instructor had got the best out of me—by creating a subtle rivalry amongst the top candidates. He'd seen my potential, and I'd earnt his respect. Did that mean Nettle's continued prickliness was mostly an act?

I didn't have time to consider the possibility any further, because Flint tossed me a saddle. Shana guided me in its positioning. I don't really understand how, but it was like I'd done it a hundred times before, and when I sat on her back, it felt as natural as if I was at the controls of my 'thopter—except way more exhilarating. I threw Flint a grin that went all the way to my eyes, and, unable to help myself, gave one to Nettle as well.

The corner of her mouth lifted, then she and Flint took off.

Shana sprang from the ledge a split-second later, and with a few powerful downbeats, we were airborne. I punched a fist into the air as I let out a victory cry. The mind-link allowed me to experience the air currents as Shana did, and I shifted my weight in synchronisation with her. It was like nothing I had ever experienced before in my life, this wordless unity.

As we banked on a thermal, circling the valley in higher and higher arcs, I marvelled at its beauty anew. The mountains, waterfall, and lake; the trees, terraces, and outcrops. All in vivid, glorious colour. But it was the cloudless blue sky above that beckoned.

Ready to catch a palyx? Flint asked, grinning even more widely than usual.

All fear had evaporated. *Absolutely!*

CHAPTER 10
NETTLE

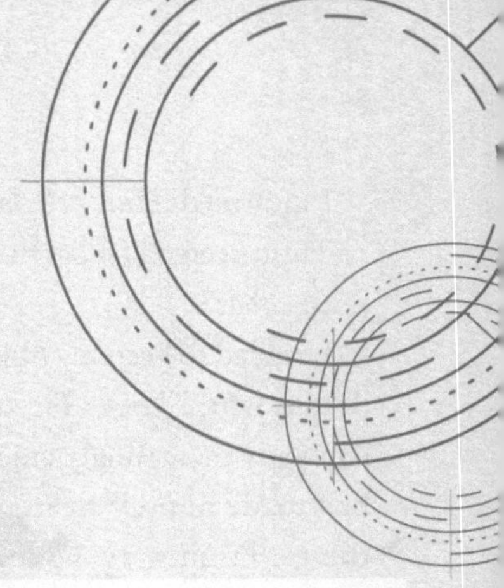

I WOULD NEVER GET sick of this feeling.

As we crested the ridge and banked, I closed my eyes and relished the simple joy of flight; of feeling one with Timu; of the wind streaming through my hair and the force of the turn pressing me into the saddle.

Opening my eyes and glancing across at Jayden, I saw his face alight with a similar exuberance.

I don't know why it surprised me. He was a pilot after all. But somehow I thought he might be clinging on for dear life, or at least have an expression of intense concentration on his face. That's how most new riders looked.

But Jayden looked like this was his hundredth ride, not his first. His position was perfect; I could tell by the sharp outline of muscles against his wind-pressed shirt. Shana took him into a barrel roll, and he whooped for joy. When he came out of it, he shot me a grin.

This is incredible!

I couldn't help it. I grinned back.

Not too shabby, fly-boy, I sent, and Timu tipped his wings in salute.

Shana took him through a few more manoeuvres, and Jayden handled them well. Fascinated, I found myself watching him... and his eyes connected with mine again. A flush of heat rose to my cheeks despite the chill of the wind, and I turned away, my stomach cinching.

Not for the first time.

I tried to pull myself together. Ok, so he was good-looking *and* a skilled flier. That didn't change anything.

Beneath me, Timu rumbled.

I squirmed. *Fine, he's decent enough. Maybe I like him.*

Timu seemed to laugh at that, and I gave him a playful slap on the neck. *Stop it!*

I needed to keep my objectivity—I was here as a second witness—but deep down, I knew Timu sensed the truth: I'd been finding Jayden's company increasingly enjoyable. He was curious and enthusiastic, and had made himself fit in, working hard and being willing to try new things. From what I'd learnt about his sister, I knew he was able to sacrifice, too, and couldn't help softening towards him as a result. I liked that he liked Flint. I liked his interest in my botanical work, and how he brought me things he knew I needed. And I liked that he wasn't scared of me.

This natural connection he shared with Shana, though... and by extension, with us... this tipped me closer to admitting more than a small degree of attraction.

If only I could fully trust him...

Hey, Nettle! Navic flowers!

Jayden's voice in my head startled me, partly because he'd mentally yelled, and partly because I'd just been thinking about him. I found him and Shana circling a section of canopy bursting with waxy, yellow blooms, and within seconds, Timu and Asha banked to join them.

They *were* navic flowers. He'd remembered the drawings...

Incredulous, I just blinked and let Timu glide.

His voice sounded in my head again, at normal volume this time. *They are, right?*

Shana had caught up to our right flank, and Jayden looked across at me, a hopeful expression on his face, just a wingspan away.

I let out a nervous laugh, though he wouldn't hear that over the wind. *Yeah, they are,* I sent. *Maybe I'll collect some on the way home. Thanks.*

Jayden beamed.

My heart raced.

Why *didn't* I trust him? Something still held me back, but maybe it was just me being stubborn.

Or scared.

The idea of a relationship with *anyone* made me nervous—vulnerability wasn't exactly my strong suit—but one with *Jayden*? I went cold just thinking about it.

As we climbed again though—Shana taking the lead with Jayden going hands-free now, his arms outstretched and leaning low—I remembered times I'd been cosy; times over the last month or so when the three of us sat in a fire circle, and Jayden's eyes had caught mine, sparkling with delight. At those times warmth had flooded me, and a desire to lean against him, have his arm drape around me... squeeze... and...

We levelled off, and Shana rolled then banked, flying back towards me. Jayden's eyes glittered as they passed, and remembered warmth flooded me, accompanied by a now-familiar swirl down low in my stomach.

I shook myself.

No. It was ridiculous. Nothing but my stupid emotions playing tricks on me.

I was here to watch Flint's back.

I'd promised my parents I would protect him... well, promised their memory anyway.

But Flint didn't really need my protection anymore. He'd made that clear.

And with him and Jayden buddying up, I'd felt a widening hole in my life.

I looked over my shoulder as Jayden swung around us again; witnessed the pure joy on his face.

My heart hitched.

Why was I fighting? Shana obviously liked him, and she was a good judge of character. She took him through a loop; zoomed beneath Asha.

Nice move! I sent, following his insane flight path with my eyes.

Reluctant as I was, I had to admit Jayden fit in here. Doc had cleared him for this final test of integration and was ready to induct him. So maybe I was being too harsh on him... or on myself.

Quite unfairly, Timu chose that moment to project into my mind the bright circles of the Balance infusing the landscape in front of us with a subliminal hum. He was reminding me of his belief that Jayden had been brought here for a reason—a reason that had to do with *me* specifically. With the endless loops of light and sound connecting everything in a great web—going through and with and in—longing and resistance battled inside me. Immediate, and almost painful.

Flint interrupted my thoughts. *Hey, Nettle, I reckon we teach Jayden how to thread.*

My eyes found his smiling ones... and the longing won.

Flint was so happy. Maybe I could be too, if I just let myself.

Sure, I told him.

With that, Timu banked first left—whipping underneath Flint—then right as Asha ducked down, cresting over the top of him. Shana joined the manoeuvre, which replicated plaiting a cord, and the three of us playfully threaded through the sky, just for fun.

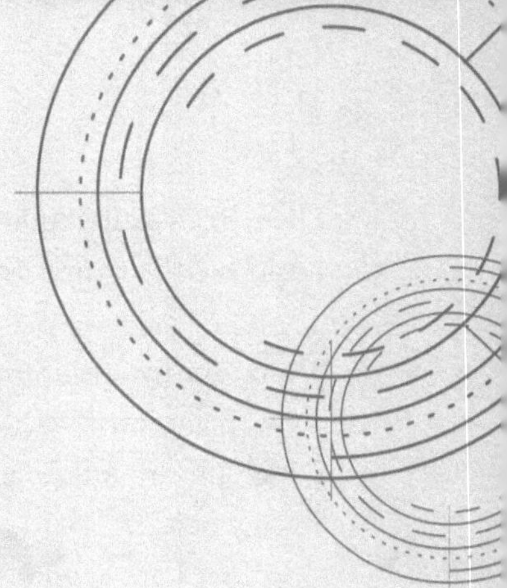

Chapter 11
Jayden

A HERD OF PALYX grazed below us. Their long, twisted horns swept back elegantly over fur that was striped on the hindquarters, reminding me of antelope, but with much longer tails.

Shana and the other Masu circled lazily overhead, hundreds of feet in the air. But despite being so far up, I could see the creatures as if I was just overhead. We'd had to fly a long way from the valley to find them, a leisurely hour or so north, but the Masu seemed to know where they'd be.

I understood why.

The creatures gave off a kind of aura—their own electromagnetic field. Grouped as they were in a herd, it acted like a beacon, albeit a jumbled up one. I'd detected smaller patches of colour as we'd soared over the trees, too. Probably the EM fields of lone animals. Now it made sense why the Masu would have this electromagnetic capability.

I'd also noted glowing circles scattered across the surface of the ground. EMP nodes? Shana rumbled beneath me as she caught onto my excitement. I realised I must have been able to sense their presence even without her—that's why I'd had the mysterious ability to avoid them in my 'thopter.

With a sound more felt than heard, one of them flared, a column of azure radiance streaming upward, and the herd separated. Not panicked, just subtly shifting position.

Did you do that? I asked Shana, but she just rumbled enigmatically. When a couple more flared though, artfully corralling the palyx, I was certain.

Then, like a bullet train hitting me, I realised what it meant: the rebels had told me the truth. The dead-zones really *were* a natural phenomenon.

Which meant oscillium operations probably *were* interfering with how this planet worked.

Which in turn meant the rebel base *wasn't* just an elaborate decoy set up for my benefit.

I lost focus, my world upended all in a moment.

You're doing way better than I expected.

I whipped my head around to face the region of sky Nettle circled in across from me, shocked to see her face alight, her aura a deep violet-blue.

Thanks, I returned, all at once glowing, perplexed, and thrown off-balance by revelations and feelings that weren't meant to be there.

Her smile morphed into that challenging one from earlier. *Now, let's see how you handle a dive.*

The glint in her eye lit me up, the thrill amplified, and I pushed aside my uncertainty. There'd be time to think about it later. Right now, all I cared about was showing her exactly what I was capable of.

Jayden! I got the image of fingers snapping in front of my eyes, and Flint joined the connection. With some reluctance, I blinked away from Nettle and focused on him instead.

You with us? Good, he said. *Now, our job is to mark a target. For some reason it makes it easier for the Masu to grab prey if there's an arrow to aim for. None of us expect you to actually hit anything, though. It takes a lot of practice.*

So, the auras were good for finding prey, but not much use for catching it. *No worries,* I replied with a nod, secretly confident.

Timu will wait for an opening, Nettle said, referring to her Masu, *then Asha will follow. Shana will probably target a breakaway, so be prepared for a sharp turn.*

I nodded again, then scanned below.

The aura of the herd was bright—almost 'noisy'—and various colours rippled through it. Mostly greens and blues. But then an area of yellow developed, and the palyx became a little skittish. Did 'yellow' mean 'alert'? Perhaps they sensed our presence.

But as I readied my bow, I noticed a few faint auras in the trees closest to the yellow section. There was something different about them. Their reddish hue was dulled; almost invisible. They moved slowly, deliberately, and one changed shape—elongating and separating into a funky 'Y' at one end. The other two soon copied it. Interestingly, the undivided parts of the 'Y's were all pointing towards the herd. The shape reminded me of something... ignited a memory...

Riflemen.

They were colonists.

A strange mixture of hope and warning blossomed in my chest. This could be my chance to escape...

Only problem was, if my attempt failed, that was it. Trust gone. No more flying.

Before I could solidify my thoughts any further, I heard Nettle whoop in triumph as her Masu came up out of a dive with a palyx gripped in its claws. A moment later, I heard shots, and Flint tumbled from his Masu just as it snatched another palyx and rose back into the air. His cry reached my enhanced ears.

The herd bolted, and the riflemen stood back up.

My stomach plummeted. *Nettle!* I shouted. Her Masu wheeled as she drew her bow. A moment later, one aura went dark.

Shana! To Flint!

Shana dove and we crossed paths with Flint's Masu, riderless and streaking in to attack. I heard shouting; shots. On the ground in seconds, I ran towards a writhing Flint. Blood stained one arm, and his breathing came in ragged gasps as he clutched at it.

Hell! What was I supposed to do?

Bandages.

I needed to stop the bleeding.

I ripped open my first aid pouch and grabbed one.

Registering a scream, I looked over my shoulder to see Flint's Masu carrying a rifleman aloft. A second later, he dropped him—but the man didn't scream this time. Already dead then. Breathing fast, I turned back to Flint. Blood oozed through the fingers covering the wound.

My mind a mess, I knelt down, grabbed my knife and cut off Flint's sleeve, then found a dressing and wrapped the gaping hole in his arm while Flint hissed in pain. The gauze was soon soaked in red. Should I make a tourniquet? Damn it, Flint was the medic, not me! Wasn't there a time limit or something before he'd lose the arm? Some vague memory from basic training screamed a warning as a whirring sound fired up in the distance.

"Flint," I said, my words tumbling through panicked breaths, "it's still bleeding. I don't know what to do."

"Just... wrap it again," Flint got out between pained gasps. "Get me... to Doc Aspen."

Nettle arrived just as I was finishing. She leapt from her Masu and ran to Flint's side, cupping his cheek with one hand and gripping his good arm with the other. "Just hang on, Flint. You're going to be ok, I promise."

I knew she couldn't promise any such thing, and so did she, because I saw fear in her eyes when she turned to look at me.

Mirroring her expression, I said, "He needs to get back to base as quickly as possible." Already, blood was seeping through the new dressing.

She gave a sharp nod. "Asha is injured. I'll take him on Timu," she said. "Help me get him up."

"Ok," I said, manoeuvring to lift Flint. "What happened with the riflemen?"

Nettle growled. "Two dead. One got away."

Timu lay as flat as possible, and Nettle and I got Flint in the saddle. He flopped along the Masu's neck and Nettle climbed up behind.

I placed a hand on her arm. Squeezed slightly. "Are you going to be able to hold him?" I asked.

She looked at my hand, then at me. "I'll be fine."

Some kind of connection crackled between us, and I longed to extend this moment, though it would be completely inappropriate. Exhaling, I stepped back, letting my hand and eyes drop.

"Jayden?"

I lifted my chin.

Nettle bit her lip. "Thank you," she said, then snapped her head forward as Timu leapt into the air and shot away at what must've been twice the speed we'd flown here at. Asha followed more slowly.

I stared after them, and as they became smaller, I let myself breathe. He'd be ok. He'd be ok.

My eyes fell on the copse of trees the riflemen had hidden in, and I looked at it, pensive.

Maybe I'd known them. I should probably check. At least bury them.

I wandered over, Shana following me. I could feel a protectiveness in her strides.

The first man was on his back with Nettle's arrow sticking out of his chest. I swallowed before moving closer, but his face was unfamiliar. He wasn't even in the military. This had been a group of filthy rich recreational hunters, by the lock of this guy's gear. Breathing a sigh of relief, I communicated to Shana that I wanted to bury him. She helped dig a shallow grave, and we slid him in and covered him up. Then, even though it seemed a stupid waste, I planted his rifle upright, in case anyone came looking for him.

The next man was some distance in—and far more mangled up. This was Asha's work, and his face was barely recognisable. I tried not to look too closely as we buried him the same way, rifle planted upright in the dirt.

As I stood up and wiped my hands on my fatigues, a strange noise caught my attention. It sounded kind of static-y, like a comm unit...

A vehicle-mounted comm unit.

Almost in a trance, I followed the sound, and found two land speeders hidden behind some bushes. The other rifleman must have got away on the third one. The comm unit buzzed again, a dull, red aura appearing around it. The garbled speech repeated a callsign, trying to get a response.

My heart started thumping.

I could answer it.

Jump on the speeder and head back to the colony. The coordinates would be programmed in.

Almost pulled, I wandered closer; touched the handlebars; ran my hands over the smooth metal, the controls, the seat.

It would be so easy.

Back to my old life; my family.

All else disappeared from my awareness. I'd wanted to go out hunting for this very opportunity. It was what had driven me ever since I'd first laid eyes on a Masu. Having now mind-linked with Shana however, I knew my plan had a fatal flaw—there was no way I could trick a Masu into helping me escape. That idea had been doomed from the start.

But now I wouldn't have to deceive her. Now, the very thing I needed to get back home had landed in my lap.

This was it. This was the answer.

And there was no one to stop me.

In slow wonder, I lifted my foot onto the mounting plate, but as I shifted my weight, Shana nuzzled me from behind. Suddenly guilty, I turned to look over my shoulder.

Her soft, green eyes regarded me. Did she know what I was thinking? I could feel her mirroring my disquiet through the mind-link.

Flint, she intimated, putting a picture of him in my mind.

Flint.

The guy who'd saved my life.

Damn.

She rubbed up against me, her gentle reprimand igniting my sense of honour. A flush of shame burned my cheeks. I realised it wasn't just Flint I'd be abandoning; it'd be Shana and Nettle too.

But wasn't it *also* the right thing to go back and look after my family? Turn their grief to joy? They didn't deserve to be abandoned either.

I grunted, now crazy mixed-up confused.

Looking in the direction I thought the colony might be in, I sighed. I'd been gone almost six months. Enough time for them to feel the pinch, but also enough time to come to terms with my 'death'.

Maybe?

Torn between my two worlds, I turned again to Shana, somehow knowing she understood. Maybe when Flint was well again, I could explain to her how badly I needed to get back and she would help me voluntarily.

For now, I think I owed it to Flint... and Nettle... to go back to base.

With a long exhale, I stepped down off the plate, took my hand off the speeder, and stroked Shana's muzzle instead. *You're right, we need to get back to Flint.*

I pressed into her, knowing she'd seen the deceit in my heart, yet had faith in me anyway.

But despite my decision, the uncomfortable confusion remained. It wasn't just Flint or Nettle, or even Shana driving it. There was something else going on.

Something I didn't want to leave behind.

Not just yet anyway.

Maybe it was selfish, but today had been exhilarating. Flying on Shana... a taste of transcendence. And I needed to consider the implications of my discovery that the rebels weren't hiding a fleet of super-powered EM shield generators.

I frowned. Did I still think of them as rebels?

I didn't know.

Regardless, now wasn't the time to leave. Flint needed me—and Nettle would be crazy with worry.

Taking one last look at the speeders, I walked out of the trees with Shana, and she flew me back to the valley.

Chapter 12
Nettle

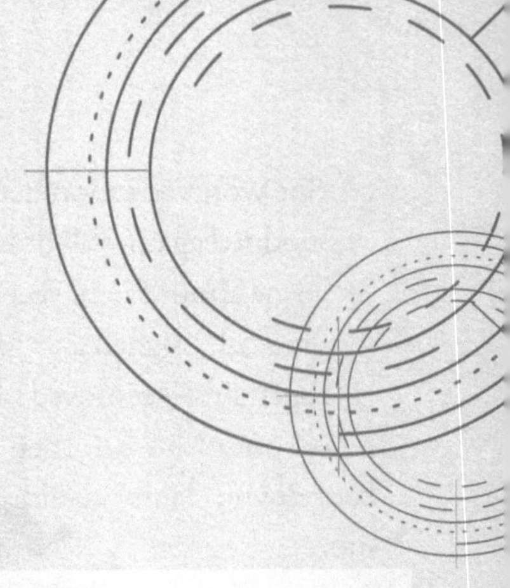

Timu had sent out a distress message as soon as we were in range of the base, so a stretcher was already waiting for Flint when we approached the wide ledge in front of the Masu den.

After flaring as gently as possible, Timu dropped to all-fours and then to his belly, flattening himself. Sure hands reached for Flint, who was barely conscious, and rolled him onto a stretcher, then carried him away before I'd had a chance to do more than squeeze his hand.

With my next breath, all the emotions I'd kept at bay during the ride tumbled forth, and, gripping Timu, I wept into his glossy fur, stained red where Flint's arm had rested.

A hand touched my back. "Can I help, Nettle?"

I turned in a rush and threw myself into Grandma Lily's arms like I hadn't done since I was a kid. "I'm so scared."

"Aspen will do his best, sweetheart," Lily soothed. "Your brother will be fine."

I wished my heart could believe her, but I nodded into her shoulder anyway. "He was shot by a colonist," I said. "Asha too..."

With that, I ripped myself out of Lily's arms and scanned the sky for Asha. I'd been so intent on getting Flint back to base, I hadn't even thought to check that the others were following us.

"If he was injured, sweetie," Lily said, "he'll take his time getting back. Coast the thermals."

Only a little reassured, I nodded mutely. "But Shana wasn't injured," I said, "so she should—"

"Knowing Shana," Lily said, "she'll stay close to Asha. Make sure he's ok. She won't abandon her cub, full-grown or not."

I nodded again, still doubtful, then turned back to Lily.

"How about I help you with Timu?" she offered.

Grateful, I sighed and gave another bob of my head.

Together, we removed his saddle. He was exhausted, so we washed the blood out of his fur, then groomed him with wet brushes to help him cool down. Timu would preen his own wings after he'd rested a little more.

Just as we were finishing up, Asha flared awkwardly and touched his rear paws to the stone. He dropped down onto only one front paw. The other he held aloft. Limping over to Timu, he licked his brother in greeting.

Concerned, I checked the paw. It needed attention, but my eyes were drawn up the slope to where Flint was no doubt being operated on.

"I'll get the vet to see to Asha," Lily said. "You go check on Flint."

The knot in my chest loosened, and I thanked her in a rush, then began to climb the path to the surgery cave, scanning the sky for Shana as I went. It was strange that she hadn't arrived with Asha, but I couldn't think about that now. I needed to know how Flint was doing.

There was a lot of rushing around when I got there, and words spoken in hushed voices.

"Clamp," I heard Doc Aspen say. "Forceps."

I bit my lip. Doc was removing shrapnel. Flint could lose the arm. He'd already lost so much blood. Maybe he wouldn't make it at all.

I hugged my arms around myself and pressed my back against the stone. No. No, he *had* to make it. He *had* to.

Someone gave me some water and I sipped it anxiously, listening to the surgical instructions. They were so calm. Detached. Finally, I put the water down and moved out of earshot. Outside on the path, one of the Masu attendants angled towards me. "How's Asha doing?" I asked.

"He'll heal up. The wound was superficial," the woman said.

"And Shana? Is she back yet?"

The woman shook her head. "No, I don't think so."

I furrowed my brow. What was taking her so long? She'd been fine.

Wandering back into the outer part of the surgery cave, I hugged my arms around myself again. Why hadn't Shana returned?

Sudden anger boiled.

Jayden.

It had to be because of Jayden.

The third colonist had raced off on his speeder, but there would have been two others.

A hollow feeling crept up my body.

Jayden had betrayed us.

Maybe even killed Shana so he could ride off on a speeder.

Back to the colony.

Clenching my teeth, I barely kept myself from screaming in rage.

I'd let my guard down, begun to trust him, when all the time he had been playing us for fools.

Tears squeezed out of my eyes, and I wanted to kick myself for falling into his trap when I'd been right from the start. I should have slit his throat when we found him. Then none of this would have happened!

Unable to remain still, but unable to leave, I paced the length of the cave, then back again, my hands balled into fists at my sides.

Why didn't I kill him when I had the chance?

Why didn't I—

"Nettle?"

I whipped around to see Jayden, concern etched on his face.

Chapter 13

Jayden

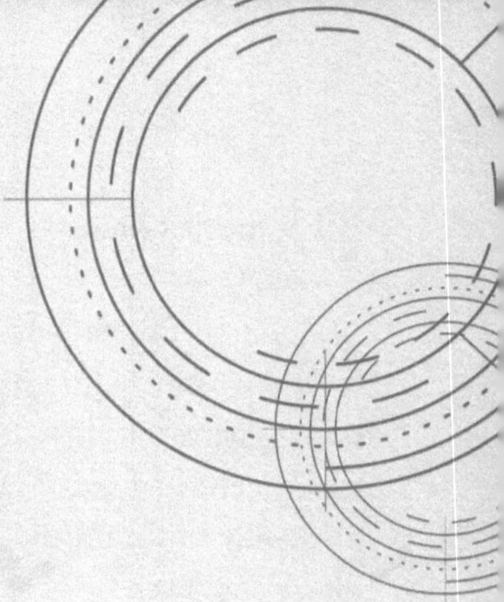

I found Nettle pacing outside the surgery cave as Doc Aspen and his team worked to save Flint's arm. I wanted to rush to her, but she looked so worked up that I just called her name.

She whipped around so fast I would have been forced to take a step backwards if I'd been much closer. There was a blaze in her eyes, but it soon turned to shock.

"How is he?" I asked.

The shock remained a moment longer, but then her eyes turned haunted. "He lost a lot of blood," she said in a small voice. "I don't know... I just don't—"

She twisted away, tears escaping from her eyes—which she quickly began to scrub at.

Before I knew what I was doing, I stepped in and pulled her close, wrapped her in my arms, and held her against me. She resisted only a second before slumping. "He'll be ok," I said. "He'll be ok."

I felt her lean her head against my chest and her body begin to shake with sobs. "I can't lose him, Jayden," she whispered. "I can't lose him too."

All I could do was rub her back, stroke her hair, while crazy, mixed-up feelings assaulted me and heat bloomed throughout my torso.

As I rested my cheek against her head, I recalled the glow I'd felt at receiving her praise.

The fear she'd let me see.

The connection we'd shared as I touched her arm.

And the way she'd said my name.

For the first time.

Ever.

And now this girl who'd always had edges as hard and sharp as gravel melted trustingly into my arms. Vulnerable, when always before she'd been so fierce.

Who else had she lost? It wasn't the time to ask. Right now, I would just enjoy this moment of softness amongst all the pain, and hope it didn't end. Ever.

"Nettle? Jayden?"

Doc Aspen's weary voice had us quickly breaking apart from each other. "How is he?" we both asked at once.

He ushered us into surgery cave, where Flint lay pale and unconscious, but alive. "I think we managed to save the arm," he said, "but he's suffering hypovolemic shock from the blood loss. If he makes it through the night, there's a good chance he'll make a full recovery, but he'll need fluids regularly when he regains consciousness."

Wanting to help, I stepped forward. "I'll sit by him," I said.

"No, I'll do it," said Nettle, joining me.

"You'll both be needed," said Doc Aspen. "You can take it in shifts. Nettle, I want you to get some rest. Jayden can sit with Flint for the next couple of hours."

"But—"

"Eat. Rest," Doc Aspen commanded. "You can do nothing for him in your current state. Look after yourself now, so you can look after him later, when he'll need you more."

I reached for Nettle's hand and gave it a squeeze. "Don't worry. I'll watch over him. If anything changes, I'll send for you."

Nettle looked like she wanted to say something, but just glanced between me, Flint, and Doc Aspen. He gave her a nod, and her anxious eyes found mine again. "Thank you."

Her gaze stayed on me much longer than it ever had before, and that warmth in my chest from earlier resurged. I felt myself drawn forward.

She looked away.

Kind of awkwardly, I released Nettle's hand. Doc Aspen took my place, putting an arm around her shoulders and walking her out with more gentle encouragement, but I remained tangled up inside as I went to sit by Flint's bed. Needing an anchor, I held the fingers of his uninjured hand. I'd always found Nettle attractive, and lately, fascinating, but what I felt now was more than that. And... did she...?

Could she...?

No... that was crazy.

Yet...

A few moments later, Doc Aspen was at my shoulder. "A word, Jayden?"

With a flinch, I twisted towards him. "Sure. Something else I should know?" I kept my tone light, but my mind was still racing.

Doc Aspen pursed his lips. "About Flint? No," he said. "But you have a decision to make."

I blinked, and my stomach dropped. "What decision?"

Doc Aspen pursed his lips again. "Whether to stay with us, or return to the colony."

What? "I... I have a choice?"

Ever since I'd arrived here, my mind had been on escape, since no one could apparently decide what to do with me, and now Doc was telling me I had to *choose* whether to stay or not?

Together with the earlier overturning of my assumptions, it just about blew my mind, but something told me that choice would disappear if I let Doc in on the truth. I'd lived a double life too long.

"Yes," Doc said, "but I'm afraid it can only be one or the other. If you leave, we expect you to stay there. It will be too dangerous to try to rendezvous."

No kidding. 'Thopters were tracked. Which brought up another question. "But won't going back give away your location anyway? The trajectory of my 'thopter would have been recorded."

"The dead-zone you crashed near was not actually the one surrounding this valley, Jayden."

"It... wasn't?" That would have been good to know earlier. "Ok then... but even so, why send me back now?"

"The skirmish today changed things," Doc said. "Or at least the time-line. For some time, I've been advocating for your integration, especially as you began to make moves in that direction of your own volition. Today was supposed to be the final test. If the Masu accepted you, the leadership hoped you would eventually become an ambassador for us, but now that our partnership with the Masu has been observed, we must act sooner than anticipated."

"Ambassador?" Lead weighed my stomach, the lie I'd lived slamming into my conscience. I was just a nobody-pilot-turned-accidental-spy who wanted to get home, collect a reward, and give his family a better life. I mean, sure, I would have reported that the rebels were no threat, that they had no diabolical plan to take over or anything, but... ambassador? That implied something more.

And it meant switching sides.

"Of sorts, yes. As I said, we can't have you going back and forth, but Central will be more inclined to believe you than any of us... and we must keep the Masu safe, as they've kept us safe. But it won't be easy either way. Still, if you're up for it, we'd be grateful."

Tangled thoughts coursed through my brain as I flicked my gaze between Doc, Flint, and nothing, lips alternately parting and closing like a fish. I ached to go home. To let my family know I was safe. Get them out of the oscillium plant.

But I also didn't.

"I... I'll think about it."

Doc Aspen nodded and put a hand on my shoulder. "Good man."

As he walked out of the room, I turned and stared at Flint. A day ago, this decision would've been a no-brainer. Mission accomplished. Now however, things didn't seem so clear. And the fact that the choice had been *offered* to me muddied the waters even more. I thought again of the speeder, and the decision I'd made earlier today.

I'd known then that I didn't really want to leave.

If I was honest, I had to admit I'd stopped collecting intel for Central months ago and... I *liked* it here. I'd learnt to make things, the food was incredible, and... I was happy. Today had merely opened my eyes to what I'd been refusing to see. Tipped the balance.

I cast my mind back to Flint's warm welcome; his genuine care for me as I recovered. The laughs we'd shared and the things he'd shown me. He was my friend now, not a naïve chump to take advantage of.

And Shana. I'd experienced a thrilling unity with her. That was a relationship just beginning; a bond I didn't want to break.

Then there was Nettle. Strong, fierce, melty Nettle. Nettle, who knew what it was like to love a sibling so ferociously you'd bust your gut for them. Intelligent Nettle, who challenged me. Vulnerable Nettle, who suffered like me.

I felt again her body in my arms... saw the way she looked at me... felt a rush to protect her... too much.

Any of these were compelling reasons to stay, but, at bottom, it came down to this: I felt like a *person* here, not just a number. Flint and Nettle had been right.

And, selfish as it was, I didn't want to let that go.

Chapter 14

Nettle

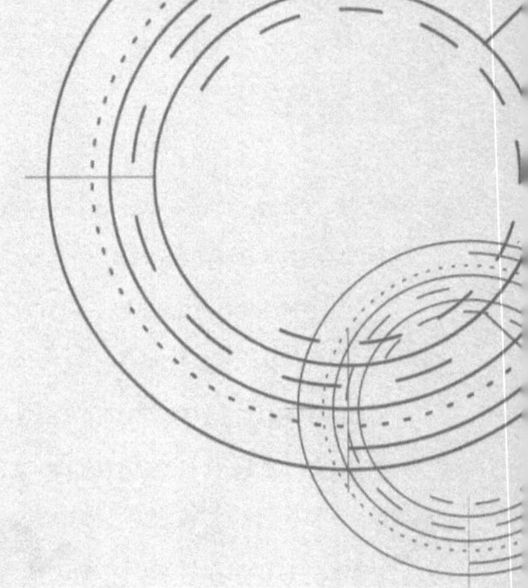

MY HEART WARRED INSIDE me as I tossed on my pallet bed.

I was trying to rest like Doc said, but I just couldn't. Too many thoughts were spinning through me, all vying for attention. There was my worry for Flint, of course, and whether he'd survive the night, regain the use of his arm, fly again...

There was my dread about what that other hunter might report, and the implications for us here in the valley...

But there was also Jayden.

How did he feel about me?

How did I feel about him?

Those two questions twisted and writhed, turning me into a complete wreck.

I had been wrong about him betraying us. I didn't know why he and Shana hadn't arrived back with Asha, but clearly he hadn't murdered her and taken off on a speeder. He'd returned. And now he was caring for Flint, just like Flint had cared for him.

And he'd held me.

Wrapped me in his arms and leant his head against mine. Rubbed my back and stroked my hair. The memory of it set that spiral of pleasure in my stomach off again. It had felt so good to be held. So good to not be alone. There'd been such comfort in leaning against his chest and releasing my fears and doubts inside the safety of his arms. I hugged myself, recreating the moment in my mind, softening its edges.

Could he have felt something too?

The way he looked at me...

I groaned. It was all so confusing! Flinging my arms out, I threw myself onto my other side.

Flint's empty bed stared back at me.

I withered inside. It was Flint Jayden cared about, not me. I was just imagining something had happened. He didn't have any special feelings for me. He'd held me because of Flint. He really liked Flint.

And he'd lost one sister, and almost another, so he knew what I was going through right now.

Yeah, that was all it was.

Still restless, I rolled the other way. My sketchbook lay open on the floor, a navic flower—bold and beautiful—spread across the page...

He'd remembered... pointed it out to me during the flight...

I reached my hand down, traced the edge of the petal like it was his cheek, bit my lip.

Jayden liked Flint, yes, but there were plenty of people who liked Flint. What made Jayden different was that he had braved my wall, and that made me feel... safe.

Safe. It was something I'd worked so hard to feel. Something that still seemed so fragile, I had to protect it by keeping everyone at arms' length.

Well, almost everyone.

But perhaps safety didn't lie in building walls anymore. Perhaps safety lay in building connections.

I hugged myself again, and a tear left the corner of one eye.

It was scary—terrifying—but right. True.

And it was time for me to be brave. Stop resisting. Let Jayden in. Like Shana had let him in.

Maybe he didn't want more with me right now, and maybe he did. Either way, I knew I wanted more with him. I wanted to be more than just Flint's sister. But I'd been pretty horrible to him for most of the last six months. Even today.

I should apologise for that.

For misjudging him.

"Tomorrow," I murmured.

With that at least settled, my restlessness eased enough for me to drift off.

Chapter 15

Jayden

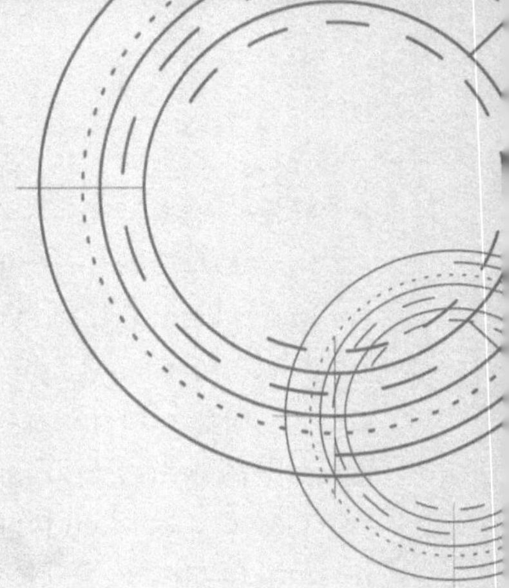

N EXT MORNING, I FOUND Nettle resting her head against Flint's abdomen and holding his hand. Her liquid eyes gazed at his sleeping face. Still not knowing what to do about Doc's question, wanting to keep my options open, and needing a gauge of her feelings for me, I sat beside her.

"How's he doing?"

"Better," she said without looking at me. "His heart-rate has stabilised, and he's sleeping peacefully now. I managed to get some more fluids into him about an hour ago. Doc seemed confident the worst is over."

I sighed in relief. He would live. Now his arm just had to heal.

"Jayden?"

Nettle had turned her eyes onto me, but they wore an expression I hadn't seen before. Going rigid, I asked, "What is it?"

She glanced down, then back up at me again. "I'm sorry," she said, biting her lip. "I misjudged you."

The tension left my shoulders. "No, don't be sorry," I said, knowing full-well her judgement was justified, but unable to let her know that. "You... you were just trying to make sure everyone here was safe. I see that now."

She gave a grim smile and a nod.

I bit my own lip. She'd given me an opening. Dare I pursue it? "You... lost someone else, didn't you?"

Her eyes fell closed and she nodded again. "My parents. They were biologists. I was seven, Flint was five. He didn't see it happen, but I..." She couldn't go on for a moment.

"You don't have to—"

"I want to," she interrupted. "I want you to know." She took a breath and started again. "Doc always saw this planet as a second-chance earth. He'd seen first-hand how we were killing ourselves in all sorts of ways and wanted to do things differently—blend old and new into a life that actually *worked*. He argued with the colony commander about it for years, especially when more and more dead-zones began appearing, but he wouldn't listen. So Doc went underground."

So far this tracked with what I'd experienced or inferred. "Go on."

"Bit by bit he collected historical schematics, information on pre-industrial processes, equipment, stores—and people. There were so many who had come here seeking a cleaner, less cluttered life, but instead found themselves constructing a replica of the existence they'd wanted to leave behind."

I wondered to myself how many of them had ended up in Wormsville.

"Just after our advance group had been secretly moved to a waystation, Central somehow discovered my parents' involvement, and the plan for the rest of us to defect within days. Soldiers came and tortured them for information, then hauled them away. I got home from school just as they were being shoved into a transport. My mother had blood on her face. I saw her silently pleading for me to run before they saw me..." Tears flowed at the memory.

I sat there, numb. What was I supposed to say? Still, I had to say something. I wanted to know her; to get close to her; to comfort her. I reached for her free hand, but didn't quite make it. "Did they? See you?"

She shook her head. "No. I intercepted Flint, and then Doc smuggled us out of the city that night with the others. He and Lily adopted us, and looked after us till we could look after ourselves."

Discomfort made me shift a little. I had a vague recollection of several people being executed around the time the rebels had left. Central said we couldn't afford to have division, or be feeding mouths that refused to work. My eight-year-old self had gone along with the crowd at the time, joining in with the insult hurling though I barely understood what was going on. I closed my eyes.

"I hate Central with every fibre of my being," Nettle said. "So when you showed up... there was no way I was going to trust you."

I opened my eyes to find her looking at me. I knew I should tell her she was right not to trust me, that I'd come here seeking a reward, and had fully intended to betray their location, but somehow, I couldn't.

"And yesterday, when you didn't come back right away, I was sure you'd taken off on one of those other speeders. But now—" A sigh cut off whatever she had been about to say next. She took a breath. "Anyway, I was wrong about you. Thank you for saving Flint."

After another breath, she closed her eyes and leant against my shoulder, her intoxicating scent filling my senses. "And... for being here... with me."

She put her free hand on my knee.

Fire exploded in my belly, a rush of desire to sweep her into my arms and kiss all the pain away—but I did none of that, just tentatively reached my arm around her back and put it on her shoulder. I knew I should tell her the truth. About the agenda I'd hidden, my plans to escape, my new desire to remain, but I... couldn't.

"Nettle?"

She rubbed her cheek against my shoulder to look up at me. "What?"

Her lips were inches from mine, and I wanted more than anything to kiss them. It looked like she wanted that too. Like I was hypnotised, I began to tilt my head and lean in...

But I would undermine our relationship before it even began if I kissed her. So the only choice I could live with involved shattering this moment. Maybe I couldn't tell her the whole truth, but I at least had to tell her about the choice I was facing—so she could decide what *she* wanted.

I heaved a breath and looked at the ceiling. "Doc Aspen told me the leadership here want me to go back to the colony as a kind of ambassador."

Nettle sat upright. "What?"

Pain jagged its way all through my chest. "He said it's my choice, but the Masu are in danger now, since someone saw us, and he thought Central might be more likely to believe me than any of you."

Nettle's eyes were wide. "So you're leaving?"

The pain twisted, constricted. "I... I haven't made up my mind yet," I said, and swallowed. "But... but protecting this place has become very important to me. Protecting the Masu, and Flint... and..."—I turned and met her eyes—"and especially you."

She stared at me in amazement, her slightly parted lips lost for words.

We stared at each other, frozen like that, for what seemed like forever, then I saw her hand drop from Flint's and reach for me.

She raised her face to mine, and, heart high in my chest, I leaned in towards her, one hand lifting to cup her cheek, the other sliding down to the small of her back.

I tilted my head.

My eyes fell closed.

I felt her soft breath meet mine...

And Flint groaned.

Loudly.

And flailed his arm a little.

Nettle's presence left me.

"I'm here, Flint," she said, grabbing his arm with both of hers. "It's ok. I'm here."

I watched her soothe him a moment, aching to receive that same tenderness from her—knowing it would be based on a foundation of deceit. One I just couldn't lay bare. Not when it might undermine achieving the only two things that really mattered.

The understanding broke me.

There wasn't really a choice. Going back would both dig my family out of their hole, and, with a bit of luck, protect everything I loved here too.

Two birds with one stone.

So why did I feel like crud?

Sighing, I stood awkwardly. "I'll go get Doc Aspen. His painkillers must've worn off."

Before I could move, Nettle twisted around and grasped my hand. "I've got more opinia-seed tincture here," she said. "Stay." Her eyes pleaded with me. Her shoulders dropped a little, and so did her voice. "Stay."

Anguish creased my brow; hollowed out my chest. "I don't think I can," I said, moving back so she had to drop my fingers, my throat closing over. "I don't think I can."

With heavy steps, I left the room.

Chapter 16
Nettle

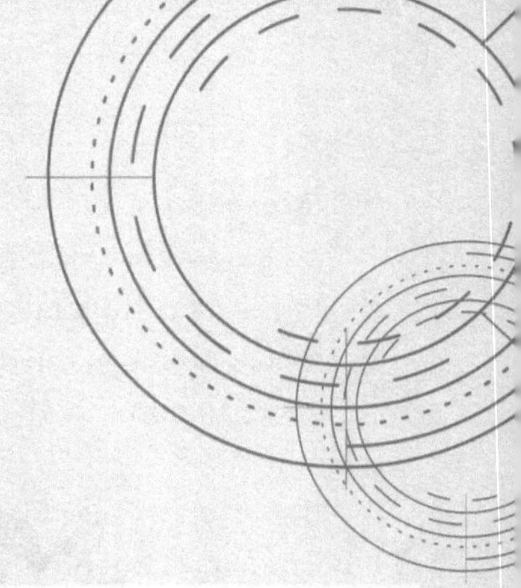

U P ON ONE OF the watch ridges, I nestled against Timu's shoulder, my mind only half on the job, and my heart feeling like lead.

I understood why Jayden had to go, and that he didn't really want to go, but that didn't make it any easier. I had found someone who loved Flint just as much as I did, someone who understood me, too—and now he was leaving.

I'd be alone again, just as I'd realised how much I didn't want to be.

I hadn't thought it possible to hate Central more, but now I did. They were robbing me *again*.

White clouds scudded across the bluest of blue skies, the Osivirian forest stretched out green and gorgeous before me, and only the sounds of birds and insects reached my ears. Any other time I would have relished a day like this, an uneventful watch just lying in the perfect dry-season sun with Timu, but today the gloom in my heart shadowed the panorama that had always delighted me.

A sudden gust beat at my back, and claws scraped on the stone. I turned to see Shana landing, Jayden on her back. His lean form slid from the saddle and wandered over to sit beside me.

"How's Flint doing?" I asked.

"Better," Jayden said.

"How're you doing?"

Jayden sighed. "Not so great."

Now we were a *pair* of gloomy storm clouds. "Yeah, me too."

We sat there in silence for a while, me leaning against Timu, Jayden hugging his knees with Shana sprawled on the other side, staring out at the vista spread before us.

"It's kind of like death, you know?" I said at last. "Like Central is taking you away from me, just like they took my parents away from me, and there's nothing I can do about it."

Jayden dropped his gaze to the space between his knees. "I know. It sucks."

"I never got revenge for the death of my parents," I said. "That's why I took my anger out on you."

He looked at me. "Nettle, it's ok, you don't have to apologise."

"I'm not apologising," I said. "I don't know what I'm doing."

There was silence for a little while longer as we both stared ahead.

"Shana showed me the Balance. You ever think about that much?" Jayden asked, still staring into the distance.

I turned a little, forehead pinched. Where had *that* question come from? "Not usually," I answered. "I have more of a... general awareness."

Jayden nodded, then looked into the distance again. "Makes sense if you grew up with it," he said. "I never used to think much about what I couldn't see, but now something deeper nudges me; calls. I guess the Masu just live inside that call instinctively."

"I guess."

To be honest, I didn't want to think about the Balance right now, when the scales seemed weighted the wrong way, though I felt Timu perk up a bit. The Masu didn't really have a concept of 'fairness' or 'unfairness', and what was happening now was most definitely unfair.

The silence stretched, and we both stared at the endless expanse of forest once more.

"I found out Asha and Timu are brothers," Jayden said after a while. "And Shana's their mother."

First the Balance, and now Masu family trees? I turned my head, wondering why, of all the things he could possibly talk about, he'd brought *that* up. "Yeah, that's right."

"But there was a third cub in the litter. A girl."

I furrowed my brows. "Timu never showed me that."

Jayden looked between his knees, then caught my eyes. "He probably doesn't remember. His sister was killed when they were very young. A giant striax python snatched her from the nest while Shana was out hunting. She found it curled up nearby with a lump inside."

Angry tears sprang to my eyes. "Did she kill it?"

"No," Jayden said, shaking his head, and there was a quality to his voice that indicated he still felt wonder at this.

"Why not?"

"She said it would hurt the Balance."

Uh huh. So *that* was the connection.

"The Masu see things differently from us. I got the impression that she understood loss as being just another part of life," Jayden went on, "and revenge a waste, resulting in nothing but two deaths instead of one. And for no purpose. She didn't need that python to feed Asha and Timu. She'd just caught a palyx, forcing the herd to regroup in the wake of their loss too. The python was being a python, just like she was being Masu. It took what it needed, just like she did. No more, no less. So she fed the palyx she'd just caught to Asha and Timu, and grieved for her daughter."

I didn't know whether I was angry or heartbroken. "Why did she show you this?"

Jayden screwed up his face a bit. "I think she was trying to comfort me."

I balked. "Did it?"

"Not really, but it made me think," he said. "The Masu are *content*, you know? And they're powerful, but they don't feel the need to prove it. Not like I do. I think Shana left that python alone because she wasn't afraid of it, and maybe she respected it. The striax pythons are their main rivals on this planet but they don't try to eliminate each other. There's not this ongoing war between them. I think there's something to learn from that."

I sighed; drooped. "Pythons aren't malicious," I said. "Central is."

"Yeah," Jayden agreed. "Humans suck like that."

There was more silence, then I pulled my lower lip between my teeth.

"Do you think you'll be able to get them to forget about us?"

Jayden cast his eyes down again. "I don't know. But I'll do my best."

I compressed my lips into a line, then squeezed my whole face up. "Damn, I wish this wasn't a one-way trip!"

Jayden took my hand. Squeezed it. "Me too."

In almost physical pain, I looked him in the eyes, internally raging at Central for tearing us apart.

Timu rubbed his head against me, and Shana rumbled and did the same to Jayden. The two of them had a remarkable bond for having been together such a short time.

Jayden kept hold of my hand, but pressed his face against Shana's and circled his other arm beneath her chin to embrace her.

And as I saw Shana nuzzle him, a dangerous thought struck me, and I wondered if I might be able to redress at least *some* of the unfairness, and give Jayden a way to come back.

Chapter 17

Jayden

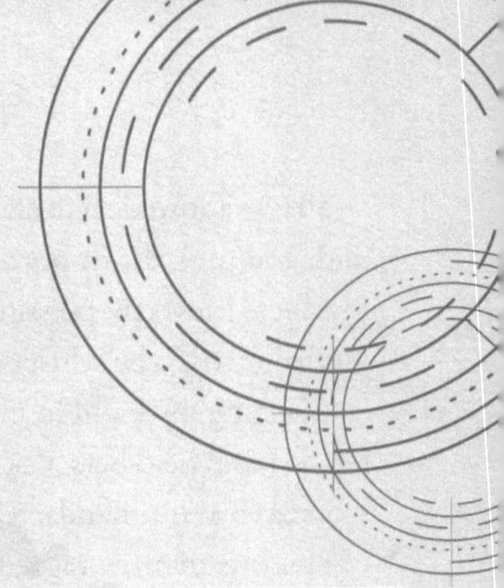

A FEW WEEKS LATER, I stood beside Shana on the broad ledge in front of the den. Two other Masu and their riders stood either side of me. Doc Aspen laid a hand on my arm and squeezed it. "Go well, Jayden. Do what you can to allay their fears about us, so our work here can continue."

I pressed my lips into a thin line, bluffing courage, and nodded. "I will."

Doc's wife Lily embraced me. "We're proud of you, Jayden," she said. "Keep them safe."

Keep them safe. The Masu, yes, but also my guides. I swallowed.

They were putting an awful lot of trust in me. I hadn't really understood just how much until now, and I really didn't know if I could live up to it. Still, I had to try.

Not trusting myself to speak, I nodded to her.

Flint approached next, his arm in a sling. "See you later, bro." With his good arm, he pulled me into a tight embrace, and I returned the pressure. "Go well," he said.

My throat felt tight. "I'm gonna miss you."

Flint smiled. "Same."

He stepped back, and Nettle took his place. Her eyes were shiny, like she'd been crying. Hating that we had to part, I moved towards her and reached for her hand. "I'm sorry."

She shook her head. "Don't be sorry," she said. "You're just trying to make sure we're safe."

The words stabbed, but I set my face stoically. "I won't forget you."

She swallowed, like she was holding back tears. "Me neither," she said, and took the opportunity to thrust herself up on her toes and kiss my cheek, covertly pressing something into my hand at the same time. "Dried miyu," she whispered, "in case you ever need it."

Clasping my hand in both of hers, she rocked back onto the soles of her feet and held herself steady.

I stared at our hands; felt the wax ball pressed inside mine.

Her breath came ragged. "Go well."

As she gave my hand another squeeze, we both understood what she really meant—*Come back*.

Leaning my forehead against hers, I breathed in her perfume, gave her hand a final squeeze, then released her fingers. Pocketing the ball as I turned stiffly, I paced over to Shana—the other girl I would be leaving behind. My bond with this matriarch of the Masu had deepened over the intervening weeks. Shana purred in delight whenever we mind-linked, and almost had a motherly air about her, instructing me like I was her own cub.

I gave her chest a stroke, then threw back the miyu infusion prepared for me. Once I'd reoriented, which now only took a second, I pressed my face into her fur once more. *I'm scared out of my mind about this*, I sent, an admission I'd made to no one else. Shana rumbled, then sent an image of me nestled in amongst her cubs as she curled affectionately around us all. She then morphed the image to give me wings, and nudged me into the air with the rest of her litter. Together, we all soared. *You can do this*, she seemed to say. But also, *I'm with you*. My whole body vibrated with her proud purring, and I felt tears welling.

Looking at me with her wise, green eyes, Shana laid herself down so I could mount her, but after scrubbing the sleeve of my old flight suit over my eyes, I first looked back over my shoulder. Solemn faces that glowed with a yellow-orange aura looked back. Despite Shana's assurances, this was a dangerous mission, and they all knew it. We would have to deliberately make contact with a checkpoint, and that might not end well.

A couple of downbeats, and the three of us were airborne, gliding over the valley I'd come to love, and was probably seeing for the last time.

We crossed the unofficial boundary into Central territory, and from then on stayed close to the canopy so we could duck below it if any 'thopters came close. My guides had already decided we'd circle round to the south in order to disguise our origin point.

Electromagnetic auras dotted the forest beneath us, and we *did* take refuge in it a few times—especially as we got closer. Soon I could see domes and towers in the distance, soaring much higher than the surrounding forest. The Masu scanned for the aura signature of a checkpoint tower, and, finding one, took us down to the forest floor before we could be sighted. My escort and I would go on foot from there.

We approached the guards at the base of the tower with upraised hands to signal we meant no harm. Even so, rifle barrels were aimed at us.

"Halt! State your name and business!"

Pushing down my fear, I took a pace forward. "Captain Jayden Seymour, 4th Airborne," I said. "Returning from a recon mission gone terribly wrong."

The guard looked at me suspiciously. "What about those two?"

"My guides," I said, heart thumping. "Leave them be. And that's 'sir' to you." Maybe I could pull rank.

"If they're rebels, we're required to arrest them," the guard said. "Sir." His tone indicated he wasn't convinced I was who I said I was.

"They brought me here in good faith," I said, feeling more and more certain this was not going to end peacefully. "Leave them be."

Lowering my chin, I put out my arms to the sides—a kind of human shield—and glared, though my stance was all bluff, my insides worse than jelly.

This was the most dangerous moment for everyone. I had wanted to approach alone, but the leadership all agreed it would be best for the colonial soldiers to see that I wasn't a prisoner. That the 'rebels' had brought me back as an act of goodwill. If I backed down now, they'd be arrested for sure, but if I didn't... the soldiers might just shoot them.

There was a tense standoff, then somewhere behind me I felt the subliminal presence of Shana. A deep tone rippled through me, and the guards' faces seemed to go blank for a second. After another moment, the one who'd done all the talking said, "Fine. We'll treat it like a hostage exchange. Advance and be recognised, Captain Seymour."

Trying not to shake, I did so, and my escorts melted back into the forest. They'd be alright now. Even if the tower sent out scouts and called in a chaser, the Masu could get them out of range before the Central soldiers even knew what was happening. I kept my face a mask, but inside, my heart still hammered. Now I was on my own.

The guard held a palm up in front of me, and I stopped short. "Retina scan," he said, "sir." He pulled out a scanner, which he held up to my eyes. Red light beamed across my face, the device beeped, and a robotic voice said, "Captain Jayden Seymour, 4th Airborne. MIA, presumed dead."

I raised an eyebrow at the guard as a subtle 'told you so', and he cleared his throat. "Welcome home, sir," he said. "We'll escort you to Central immediately."

"Captain Seymour, it's good to have you back alive."

In his sharp grey uniform accented in red, Colony Commander Tun shook my hand at the door to his office.

I returned the pressure, burying my nerves behind military discipline. The man was enormous. Half a head taller than me at least, and far broader. "It's good to *be* alive, sir," I said, entering the generous, semi-circular space behind him.

While I stood, staring through the curved glass frontage at the commanding view of the city below and forest beyond, he paced to his desk, booted heels clicking on the large, white tiles that spanned most of the floor. The sound of them stopped when he reached the carpeted area beneath the heavyset wooden monolith. I turned to face it. Polished plaques, medals, and trophies lined the wall behind, and a lone potted plant arched its fronds to one side.

Tun cleared his throat. He was seated at the desk now, and indicated the chair on the other side of it to me. Feeling like a child caught stealing from the sugar ration, I took it.

"You're the first to come back from a crash landing in a dead-zone, you know that?" His silver hair glinted a little as he tilted himself back in his chair. "Most of those who went after the reward balked at the EM barriers, and those who didn't..."

I drew myself up. Acted important. "I was lucky, sir," I said. "And lucky to be found by those you call rebels."

Commander Tun raised an eyebrow. "You don't call them that?"

"They're harmless, sir," I said, stomach beginning to knot. "They seek only to live off the land, and make sure the colony survives long-term. I was given medical attention and treated as a guest among them. They have no weaponry beyond what they use to hunt—knives, bows, spears—and practice ancient pre-industrial crafts and biodynamic farming. There is no need to bother with them. They are no threat to the colony."

Tun leant forward, palms flat on his desk. "Then why the hell do they need those off-the-scale EM shields, Captain?" His eyes were hard; his jaw fixed. "The ones that cause my 'thopters to crash and mining equipment to shut down?"

Maintaining my act, I took a centring breath. "They're a natural occurrence, sir, most likely exacerbated by our disturbance of the oscillium reserves," I said. "A combination of geological factors, frequency amplification to the point of destructive resonance, and the concentrated presence of a particular type of creature."

We'd gone over and over what I should say to this question a hundred times, and I still wasn't sure whether it was a good idea to admit anything of the sort.

"The flying cats?" he asked.

Damn, he'd put two and two together very quickly. "They're called Masu, sir."

Tun narrowed his eyes at me. "You seem awfully fond of these... 'masu', Captain."

I lifted my chin a bit, though my insides screamed danger at me. "With all due respect, sir, it's hard not to be. If not for them, I wouldn't be alive right now."

The colony commander tilted his head a little, and one corner of his mouth lifted in a smile. "Of course."

Into the silence that followed, I scrambled for one final statement. Just to make things crystal clear. "If you want to stop the dead-zone expansion, sir, you need to cease oscillium operations," I said. "The rebels aren't generating anything."

Tun examined me a moment, then said, "I see."

I wasn't sure he did, but I was walking a knife-edge here already, torn between a sense of duty to both of my families. Saying much more could get me locked up as a rebel sympathiser, and that wouldn't help anyone.

The colony commander drummed his fingers on the desk for a few beats, then rose and extended his hand to me. I stood and grasped it.

"Well," he said, smiling, "intel will want your full debrief, and then I believe you've a reward to collect, Captain, and a family to reunite with. Thank you for your report. It's been highly illuminating."

"You're welcome, sir," I said. "And thank you."

I stood to attention, and Tun squared his shoulders and gave a sharp nod.

But I left his immaculate office with its endless view of Osivirius feeling that something terrible had just happened, and I had no idea what.

Chapter 18

Nettle

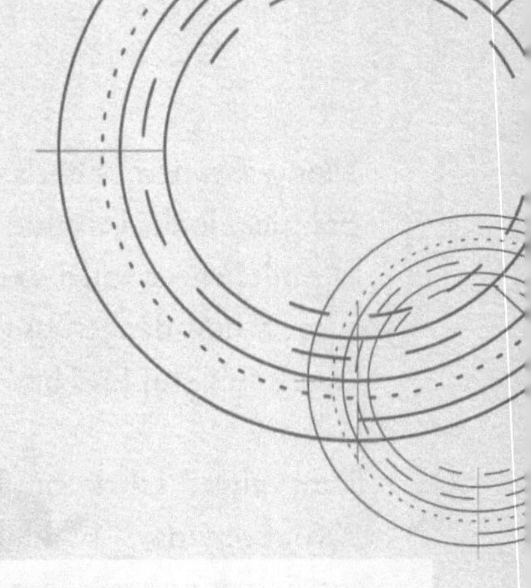

Two weeks had passed since Jayden had left. Flint's arm had healed, and we were down in the garden picking medicinal herbs as part of his rehab routine. A flight of Masu came in to land overhead.

"Do you remember when we took Jayden here for the first time?" Flint asked me.

"Yeah," I replied with a sad smile.

"I wonder how he's doing?"

I sighed. "He's doing ok."

Flint narrowed his eyes at me. "How do you know?"

Crap.

"Well, I *guess* he's doing ok," I said, trying to cover my tracks. "I mean, he's the kind of guy that does ok. And he's back with his family."

Flint's chin lowered. "I know you, Nettle," he said. "And that's not what you meant. What are you hiding?"

A storm began circling in my middle, but I turned away and stayed quiet. Picked a few sprigs of lanya.

"Nettle?"

Damn. He wasn't going to drop it, and no plausible lie presented itself to me. I'd just have to tell him the truth. "Shana's been keeping an eye on him," I admitted in a murmur.

"What?" Flint exploded.

I glared at him. "Keep your voice down!" I hissed.

Flint bent low beside me. "Are you telling me you sent Shana to the colony?"

"No!" I snapped. "I *asked* her. And she said yes."

"You *asked* her?" Flint's voice was loud again.

Frantic, I looked around surreptitiously. "Flint! Quiet!"

"I can't believe you'd *do* that, Nettle," Flint whisper-shouted. "Don't you know how dangerous that could be for Shana?"

"She's not stupid, Flint," I said, ripping out lanya. "And it was her decision."

Flint calmed a little, but his brows stayed down. "Still... every *day*?"

"Not every day," I said, keeping my head down. "And she flies in at night. Sometimes tails him when he goes out in his 'thopter."

Flint shook his head. "I still find it hard to believe she'd do something like that."

I tried to look nonchalant as I continued my work. "She really likes Jayden," I said with a shrug. "She says there's something special about him. Something different. He sees more."

Flint screwed up his face. "What's that supposed to mean?"

I was so ready to end this line of questioning. Face hard, I met Flint's eyes properly. "I don't know, but the point is she wants to do this, so just drop it, ok?"

On edge again, I moved onto plucking opinia, my movements aggressive.

Flint watched me, and his movements slowed. "There's something else, isn't there?"

I stopped mid-pluck.

"Isn't there?" Flint pressed.

Damn. I probably shouldn't have been so touchy. I bit my lip. "I gave Jayden some dried miyu."

Flint just about bolted upright. "You what?" he whisper-shouted again.

"Shhh!" Pulling at his sleeve, I looked around in terror, desperately hoping no one was paying attention to us.

Flint leaned close. "You do know how dangerous that is, right? What if he tries to use it? What if someone finds it? What if he's followed?"

All things I'd considered. "He's not stupid enough to use it before

Shana makes herself known... and... and I trust him. Don't you?"

Flint was silent, then his face cleared. "You want him to come back."

My throat constricted, and I turned away. "Of course I want him to come back... eventually."

Flint sighed.

I turned back to him, eyes pleading. "Don't say anything. Please."

Flint pursed his lips. Mulled it over. Sighed again.

"Fine."

Chapter 19

Jayden

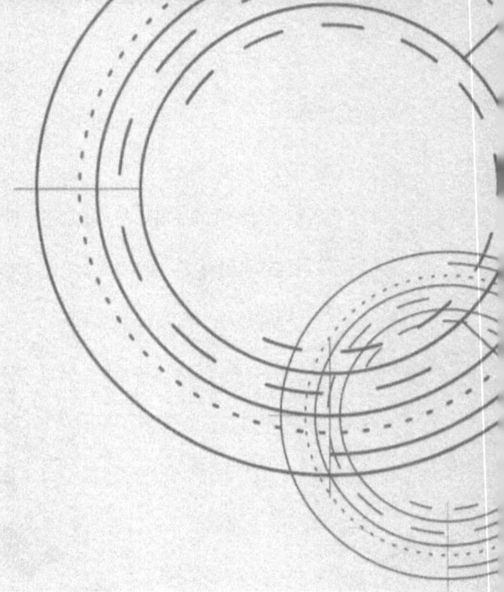

A MONTH HAD PASSED. I sat facing the panoramic view from our forty-first-floor apartment, pushing oatmeal around my bowl. My feet brushed soft carpet, I wore a soft cotton robe, and I had woken up from a bed that had a soft duvet and pillows.

Half a year ago, this had been everything I wanted, but now I'd give anything for the chance to step on woven palm mats and scoop the tart sweetness of gupi fruit into my mouth. Feeling kind of dead, I rested the spoon on the side of the bowl and pushed it away. Then, of their own accord it seemed, my fingers reached into my pocket and rolled the little wax ball I always kept with me.

But this was a prison I'd have to stay in.

My sister Sarah padded across the living space to the kitchen and made herself a cup of sim-coffee. "Wanna join me for AR skirmish this evening? It's Bio-5 versus Bio-4 in a city-wide tournament. Should be awesome."

I shrugged. "Maybe."

Once I would have jumped at the chance, but what fun was augmented reality when there was a *real* reality out there? If I couldn't be a part of it, I just wanted to disengage from everyone and everything.

"What's up, Jay?"

I glanced over at Sarah, so contentedly sipping the simulated garbage that streamed out of a tap in our sleek kitchen straight into her mug. This life was wild for her, so different from the cramped, dim, sterile box we used to live in. Well, not the sterile part. This apartment may have a glass frontage, plush lounges, and tasteful décor, but it was still sterile.

And not nearly wild enough for me.

"Nothing," I said. "I gotta get ready for work. See you later."

"Ok. See you later."

Pulling the bowl towards me again, I scooped the last bit of sludgy oatmeal into my mouth and took it to the kitchen, where a domesti-bot set about cleaning it. The spoon, I kept. It was the wooden one I'd carved myself, and I washed it in the bathroom as a tiny act of rebellion in this pampered existence.

Flight suit and boots on, I left my room. My mother met me in the hall. "My hero wasn't going to sneak off without giving me a hug, was he?" she asked with a smile.

"Whatever gave you that idea?" I asked, feeling slightly guilty, and nothing like a hero. "I just have an early start today."

My mother twisted her mouth, unconvinced. "You haven't seemed happy lately, Jayden. Anyone would think you missed our little underground box."

"It's not the box I miss," I mumbled.

"You miss the rebels?"

The anger I'd buried surged up. "How many times do I have to tell you they're not rebels?" My voice was harsher than I meant it to be. "Sorry."

My mother pressed her lips into a line, then drew me into an embrace. "Have a good day, Jayden."

I grunted something indistinct, then pushed the button that opened the apartment door. It slid aside in swift efficiency, then closed itself behind me. Another few steps and I was zooming down the elevator tube to the air-bridge level and making my way across to the 'thopter hangars. Would I fly a surveillance mission today? Or run supplies to a logging or mining facility? Did it matter? Every mission brought an ache to my heart, and I kept on thinking I saw Masu in my periphery, which made me a million times more aware of what I was missing out on. I had hoped to at least be showing scientific or agricultural teams what I knew of the plant life of Osivirius, but they lost interest in me soon after I told them that the dead-zone I'd crashed in wasn't actually the one surrounding the base. No one in Central had seemed much interested in learning about anything actually *useful*, when earth seeds grew just fine and drugs were easy enough to synthesise.

Fools.

I glanced around me. The wide, silvery air-bridge arced across the space between towers, about a hundred feet up. Below, I could see a few city-skimmers zipping along the roadways, but only a dozen or so people moved about the grey, concrete landscape. I looked upwards. Lines and angles soared to the sky, sleek and reflective; the precise, sophisticated curves of the four crystal towers and Central's intimidating spire balancing the more utilitarian monoliths and puffing chimneys. The enormous hex-frame bubbles of the biodomes rose in the middle-distance, and beyond them spread the green expanse I longed to be in.

I tore my gaze away, sent it to the concrete below my feet, and listened to the swoosh of vehicles and the tap of my boots, trying not to think about the raw beauty of the valley. It was easier to be numb.

Soon enough, after making my way down several levels, my hangar loomed: a great, yawning arch, ready to swallow me. At this hour, only a few mechanics and refuellers wandered about in its great maw. Frozen at the threshold, I darted my eyes around, debating where to go next. I didn't really want to be here. I just wanted to be in the apartment even less. Maybe I should turn around and pretend I'd forgotten something.

Yeah, that'd work.

"Hey," said a smooth voice behind me. "How's Captain Back-From-The-Dead this morning? Here bright and early for another glorious day in civilisation?"

It was Major Reynolds, our squadron commander. I gave him what I hoped was a convincing smile.

He put his arm around my shoulder and leaned in conspiratorially. "Word on the street is we're bringing some stray lambs back into the fold soon—thanks to you."

Alarm bells rang inside me, and I blinked. "Sir?"

He winked. "You'll find out all about it in the Operation SHEP-

HERD briefing at 0900."

There was a buzz in the briefing room as I took my seat. Externally, I kept a neutral face, but my insides were roiling. What the hell was Central planning—and why?

Major Reynolds called for silence.

"Fifteen years ago, our colony suffered a terrible blow," he began, "when a small but powerful segment broke away, leaving us without vital skillsets, resources, and labour. But we rallied, we survived. And despite their attacks on us, despite the inventory and the good people we lost, we never gave up."

There were murmurs of agreement around the room, but the major held up a hand so he could continue.

"It's time to bring these lost sheep back home, people." He smiled and spread his arms. "Thanks to Captain Seymour here"—he gestured towards me and I struggled not to shrink back—"we know these non-conformists don't have a weapon to their name worth worrying about if we take them on the ground. And it seems they *have* been working hard whilst they were gone, and have a nice little farm going."

He again smiled ingratiatingly.

"We're taking over production," he stated, "and securing our oscillium holdings at the same time."

A few murmurs.

"That's right people," he continued. "Not only will the shepherd once again have a united flock, but direct action now should stop any more dead-zones from popping up—and maybe even cause some to disappear."

Excited murmurs now, but for me, a deepening sense of dread.

Reynolds took up a slim, white pointer and tapped the wall map.

"Over the past month, we've narrowed down the possibilities and are fairly certain which of the EM walls the rebels are hiding behind. We just have to tighten the noose. In three days, our airborne units will begin to transport ground troops to strategic locations. Once everyone's in place, it'll be a simple matter of shooting down any flying cat we see. With the kitties gone, the rebels'll have no choice but to surrender, and we can walk right on in."

My insides shrivelled. No. No. This couldn't be happening. I struggled to keep my breathing under control, my body relaxed and alert, but I knew my eyes showed more white than usual, and my limbs stiffened.

Central wanted to exterminate the Masu and turn the paradise I loved into another one of their factories, on the off-chance they could keep mining oscillium with impunity.

The major took questions from the floor, but I didn't hear any of them. Time seemed to stop for me. I imagined Flint and Nettle being prodded forward by rifle barrels, Shana's aura flickering out as she died, machinery rolling into the valley.

I had to warn them.

I had to stop this from happening.

And I had to do it today.

Chairs scraped on the floor as people stood to leave. Shocked from my daze, I stood too. I was almost through the door when Major Reynolds called out, "Captain Seymour, a word, please."

I stiffened. Was the game up before I'd even arranged the cards in my hand? Schooling my features, I turned around as the last person went through the door. "Sir?"

Major Reynolds cocked his head at me. "You good?"

What was I supposed to say? The truth would land me in the brig, but acting eager would also be suspicious. "Fine. But is this truly necessary, sir? I thought Central was only worried the rebels were planning an attack. I was pretty clear in my debrief that they weren't, and I have my doubts about the dead-zones disappearing too."

He gave me a penetrating look. "This was never about an attack, son," he said. "The price of oscillium and the other minerals we mine here has gone down. To stay viable, we have to lower production costs. In any way possible. We simply can't afford any more dead-zones randomly popping up, and we need every single person we've got working. The intent of the rebels is by-and-large irrelevant. Dissent is not something that can be tolerated, and, natural or not, neither can anything that gets in the way of production."

I kept my face a mask. Credits. It always came down to credits. "I suppose not, sir."

He sighed. "Let's just hope the rebels do the smart thing and cooperate."

My stomach clenched, a ball of anger churning inside it, but I kept it hidden. "They're very smart people, sir," I said.

"They were some of our best," Major Reynolds said with a sigh. "Scientists, engineers, chemists, medical personnel. That's what made it such a slap in the face. Colony Commander Tun lost his grandkids because of their betrayal. Had to execute his own son and daughter-in-law as a warning too. That's not something a person can forgive easily."

So, this was personal.

Well, it was personal for me too.

But how was I going to do it without being caught? Without being branded a rebel myself?

And what would my own family think?

Questions for later. Right now, I had to look like I was onboard with the plan. "I understand, sir," I said.

"Good man," he said. "If you have any influence among them, make sure you use it."

I nodded. "Don't worry, sir," I said. "I will."

Just not in the way the major hoped.

Chapter 20

Jayden

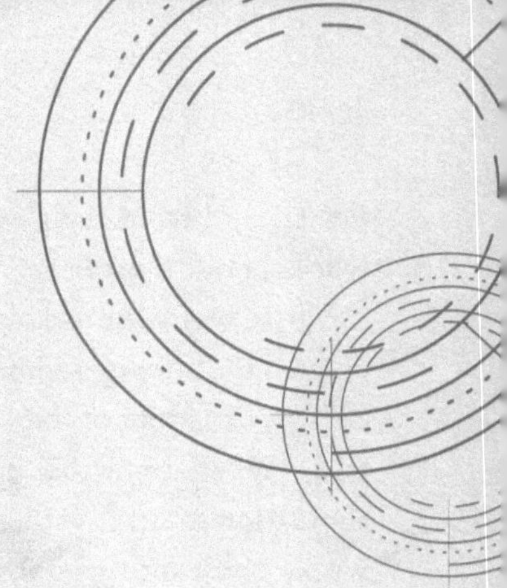

"**E**ww! What's that smell!"

Damn. I didn't want Sarah to be suspicious. I capped the vacuum flask in a hurry as she strode over to the kitchen. "I burnt something. Don't worry about it," I said.

Sarah rolled her eyes. "C'mon, Jayden, let the domesti-bot handle the cooking. We're not poor worms living underground anymore. Enjoy the benefits!"

I lowered my gaze; curbed my ire. "I just like doing things myself, that's all."

Sarah twisted her mouth into a smirk. "You never were content to let other people handle things, were you?"

"And where would we be now if I had?"

Sarah shrugged. "Fair point."

I quickly changed the subject. "Hey, your crew still having that AR tournament tonight?"

Sarah's eyes lit up. "Absolutely. You coming?"

"Sure," I said. "I could use the distraction."

Literally.

Half an hour later, I entered the AR venue to get myself kitted up. Like everyone else, I wore dark coveralls, and got issued a tracking dot to stick on my sleeve, an AR headset, and a sim-weapon.

Unlike everyone else, I'd had a tiny sip of miyu infusion. My senses hadn't exploded in power like when I was paired with Shana, but they were still incredibly sharp. There'd been a little bit of wooziness to break through, but then I saw faint EM auras around everyone and any active device, and from the elevated walkways, glowing patches of ground where a node must be.

There was a lot of laughter amongst the thirty or so people as we entered the briefing room.

"Ok, first event of the evening is scavenger survival," the game-master said. "We're gonna dial up the heat and drop some monsters into the simulation to make gathering your items just that little bit harder. The whole city's up for grabs as far as boundaries go, and you can take subways, transports, or city-skimmers, but you've only got one hour to acquire the items on your list and meet back here. Scores are based both on how many items are found, and how many people make it back here within the time-limit alive. You have five minutes for a team huddle, and your time starts when you hear the buzzer. Let's skirmish!"

I couldn't have asked for a more perfect scenario. The whole city to dart through without being questioned, and no one from the opposing team hunting me. The list of items appeared as a projection on our headsets, but I didn't even look at it, and only half-listened to what was going on in the huddle. I had my own strategy to work out.

The buzzer sounded, and we all crowded into the elevator tubes, barrelled out into the foyer, and were confronted with our first monster—a giant disembodied maw with a frighteningly large array of teeth. The entirety of Bio-4 and Bio-5 opened up on it, and the simulation flickered out.

"This way," whispered Sarah, and pulled me towards a side door no one else seemed to have noticed.

We entered a dingy alleyway, and I checked for monsters. Those were going to be my main obstacles. If one 'killed' me, I would be expected to return to base. A screech sounded overhead, and something like a pterodactyl dove towards us. Our sim-weapons clicked as we shot at it, and it disintegrated into pixels.

"I'm gonna head for the subway," I said.

Sarah frowned. "We should stick together."

"We can collect more items if we separate," I said, already running.

"We can protect each other if we don't," Sarah panted, sprinting after me.

I grit my teeth a little. Fine. I would just have to lose her somewhere.

I noticed a little electromagnetic flare-up in the lenses of my headset just before a new monster appeared at the bottom of the subway stairs. Excellent. I had a way of anticipating them.

The carriage was half-empty as we jumped in, and very few of the exhausted passengers paid any attention to us whatsoever. I stuck my tracking dot onto one of their bags as we got off near the perimeter wall. This was familiar territory now. The 'worm-zone' we used to live in. I spied another node.

"What were you planning to collect here?" asked Sarah as we ran up the stairs to ground level, shooting at another monster that appeared.

"Uh, a leaf," I said, quickly scanning the list. "They blow in over the perimeter wall."

But I didn't look for a leaf. Instead, I darted towards an alley from where I could observe the gate security. One guard was at ground level, and two were atop the wall itself, but they were focusing their attention outside the city. I somehow had to convince the one on the ground to let me out—that or knock him unconscious and steal his access card.

"Got one," Sarah said, appearing beside me. "How about we try for a belt next."

I kept my eyes fixed on the guard. "Yeah, sure, you go ahead," I said, hardly even hearing her.

"Why are you watching that security guard?" Sarah said, but before I could answer, a flash in my AR glasses alerted me to the presence of another monster. I whipped around and shot it, then went straight back to my surveillance.

"Jayden?"

I glared at Sarah. "What?"

"Why are you staring at that security guard? Are you hoping to steal *his* belt?"

Damn. Why wouldn't she just go away? "No."

"Then let's go. Somebody in Wormsville might loan us one."

"You go," I said. "I need to do something here."

"What?"

I let out a blast of breath. She wasn't going to leave me alone, was she? I could try and lose her in Wormsville, then circle back here, but I could sense her growing suspicion, and was pretty sure that wouldn't work.

That left telling her the truth.

Would she try to stop me? Report me?

Did it even matter? Once through the gate, I'd have five minutes tops before some kind of alarm was sounded.

"Look, Sarah," I said. "I've got to get out of here. Something terrible is happening, and I need to warn my friends."

Sarah's mouth fell open a little. "Are you *crazy*, Jayden!" she hissed. A second later she was disintegrating a monster, but soon turned angry eyes on me again. "What about *us*? Don't you care about *us*?"

I grit my teeth. Growled. "Of *course* I care about you! But you're not in danger of dying. They are. So please, either help me, or leave me to my fate, because I can't just stand by and watch an entire species be exterminated for the sake of a few credits!"

I could feel the heat behind my eyes, the sick feeling in my stomach, the tension in my chest and arms. My breaths came heavy as I watched a series of emotions flicker across my sister's face.

"You're an idiot," she said. "A selfish *idiot*." With that, she spun on her heel and stalked down the alley.

I deflated, her words cutting me more than I wanted to admit. I guess I'd secretly hoped she would jump on board, and we'd do this together, like we'd always done things together as kids, but she was a different person now. Just like I was.

After taking another breath, I turned my attention back to the guard. He was absently fiddling with his access card, pulling it out on the retractable string attached to his belt and letting it snap back. He looked fairly young, so what I had in mind might just work. If not, well... there was always Plan B.

Keeping to the shadows, I circled around and approached him at a run along the perimeter wall. "Buddy!" I called, feigning panic. "Buddy! Help me out, will you? The game-master's set a titan of a monster after me, and I need a few minutes for my weapon to recharge. Let me out the gate, will you? Just till it passes by? I'm toast otherwise."

One corner of the guard's mouth quirked up. "You know I can't do that, mate. It's dangerous out there."

"Please," I begged, "it's only for a few minutes. You know what it's like in skirmish! I'm *this* close!" I held my thumb and forefinger about half an inch apart, then checked over my shoulder.

"Look, I'd like to help, but—"

A scream distracted us both.

It was Sarah, just feet away. She shot me a meaningful glance, then continued faking some sort of injury or distress.

"Are you ok, miss?" the guard asked, right as I used his distracted state to zip his access card over the reader plate.

"No," Sarah panted, as the door latch clicked and I eased the card back towards his belt, mouthed 'thank you', and slipped through, ripping off my headset as I went. Her gasps of phony pain cut off as the door closed behind me.

As silently as I could, I ran close to the perimeter wall until I was a decent distance from the checkpoint and the road to its associated tower. Hoping that the wall-top guards had also been distracted by Sarah's show, I sprinted across the cleared area and into the forest beyond.

Just as I reached the trees, an alarm sounded, and spotlights flared to life.

I put on a burst of speed and kept running.

Beams of light criss-crossed beside me, above me, around me, but I tore through the trees as fast as I could go. I heard the pop of small-arms fire, and a few random shots hit trees alarmingly close to where I was. Soon 'thopters would be scrambled and foot soldiers dispatched from the nearby towers. I was staking *everything* on the next part of my plan working, but there were no guarantees.

I kept running till I could run no more, then found the biggest tree I could with a node nearby and leant on the far side of it to catch my breath. *Please, let that phantom Masu be real.*

Taking the vacuum flask with my miyu infusion from my backpack, I looked at it and swallowed, suddenly doubting myself. A tiny bit of miyu enhanced the senses, but I didn't know what taking a full shot of it would do if there was no Masu to catch me. Maybe I'd fall in a dead faint, have a seizure, lose my mind like Vine...

I had to try anyway.

My hands shook a little as I poured a shot into the lid of the flask, whether from exertion or fear, I couldn't tell. It was probably both. The pungent liquid still steamed a bit, but after stepping onto the azure node and counting to three, I threw it back.

The bitter brew seared my throat as it always did, its now familiar effects sending me into a dizzying swirl. *Help!* I sent out. *If there are any Masu here, please, catch me!*

I spun in an empty void, unable to feel my body.

Forever...

... and forever...

... and forever.

Sleepy, woozy, my mind beginning to blur, I continued to call for a mind-link. *It's Jayden... it's Jayd...*

Tumbling in blackness, even my mental tongue a swollen thing, I felt myself jerk in the throes of losing consciousness. This was it. It was all over...

Jayden.

With a tingle of subliminal sound, a stronger consciousness swept me up. *Shana?*

The Masu wrapped me in her comforting presence and my senses became sharp once more.

My face in the dirt and the sound of 'thopters in the distance were the first things I registered. Pushing myself to my knees, I looked around, but Shana wasn't there. I got up and kept moving further into the forest.

Now that we were linked, she could find me, and I wanted to be as far away from the colony as possible when she did.

I sensed her getting closer, the bond strengthening, then she was there, and I hauled myself onto her bare back. This was going to be one hell of a ride without a saddle, but I trusted her.

Why're you here? I asked as she sprang into the air.

Shana put a picture of Nettle in my mind.

What? Damn... Nettle had asked her to stay in the area and she *had*, despite how dangerous that was.

In response, Shana put an image of her defending Asha and Timu into my mind.

Ok, so it hadn't *just* been Nettle's request that had made her stay. Shana cared, and somehow, she'd known I'd need her.

I closed my eyes and pressed my cheek against her neck. *Thank you.*

We skimmed just above the treetops, the searchlights of the 'thopters visible behind us. Shana veered south and ducked below the canopy, waiting for them to fly past. When they had, she followed behind them. *Smart girl.* I clung to the fur of her neck and let her navigate back to the valley. We passed through the EM barrier, floated over the ridge, and began our descent. The waterfall sparkled in the moonlight, and reflected stars twinkled in the lake's surface, wild and beautiful. It felt like coming home.

The night watch coordinator met us on the ledge. "Jayden? What are you doing here?"

"Gather the leadership," I said, sliding off Shana's back. "Central is planning an attack. I came to warn you."

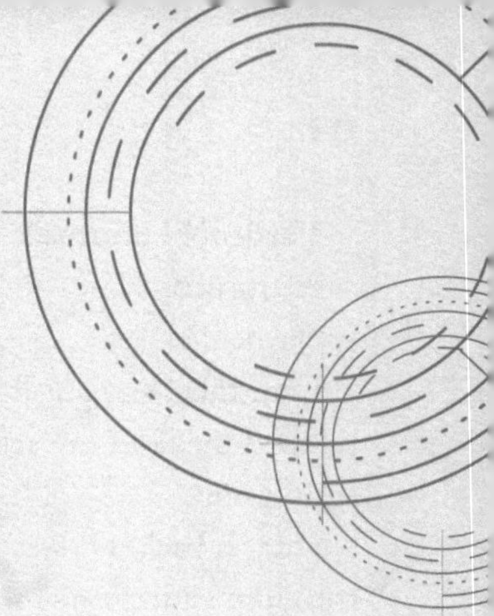

Chapter 21
Nettle

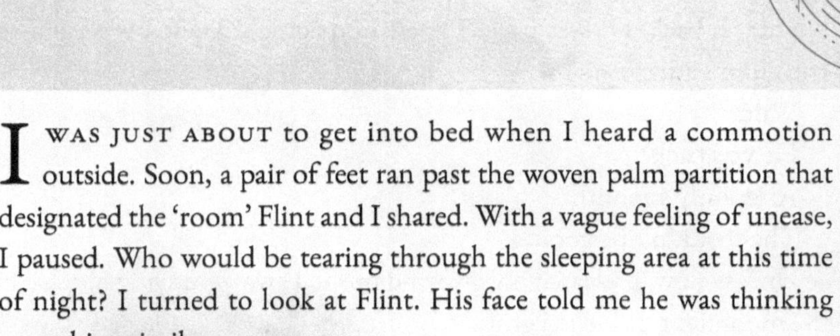

I WAS JUST ABOUT to get into bed when I heard a commotion outside. Soon, a pair of feet ran past the woven palm partition that designated the 'room' Flint and I shared. With a vague feeling of unease, I paused. Who would be tearing through the sleeping area at this time of night? I turned to look at Flint. His face told me he was thinking something similar.

I peeked through the split in the palm matting. In the dim light, I saw the runner scratching on a door further along. One of the senior engineers poked his head out, and he and the runner had a hushed conversation. The engineer nodded, then ducked back behind the partition, emerging a few moments later with his boots back on. Then he and the runner disappeared further inside the cave.

"They're gathering the leadership," I whispered to Flint. "Something's going on."

"Have you heard from Shana?" Flint whispered back.

"No," I said. "She left for the colony a few hours ago."

That vague unease deepened to dread. We shared a look, then both of us hauled our fatigues over the top of our pyjamas and pulled our boots on.

Slipping out into the 'corridor', I snuck towards the cave entrance, Flint following me.

We rounded a curve, and he rammed into the back of me as I pulled up short.

There, silhouetted against the moonlight, was a figure I'd recognise anywhere.

"Jayden?" I breathed.

He turned.

"Jayden!"

I ran then, straight into arms held wide for me. Their strength enveloped me, and my arms were equally forceful as I crushed myself against him.

He was back! He was back! I knew he'd come! I knew I was right to trust him with the miyu!

Wait...

He was back?

After only a month?

That couldn't be good.

Uneasy now, I released my grip and pushed away, studying his face in the moonlight. It looked grim.

"Something's wrong, isn't it?" I asked, spikes of fear crawling up my spine.

He nodded. Swallowed. "Yeah. The Masu are in danger. You're all in danger," he said. "I'm briefing the—"

"Jayden?"

Doc's voice sounded behind me. With a final tense look, Jayden released me completely and stepped sideways. As his hand brushed across my back, I swung around to face Doc.

"Good heavens, it really is you."

Jayden bobbed in a kind of half bow. "There've been some developments. I have to brief the leadership team immediately."

Doc didn't appear to hear. "How did you get here?"

"Long story," said Jayden, and I shifted uncomfortably. "But there are more important things to discuss."

By now, the other members of the leadership team had appeared, and Jayden acknowledged them with nods.

I squirmed. Flint cleared his throat.

Doc compressed his lips into a line, and his brows furrowed. "Very well," he said. "Come along then. Good night, Nettle; Flint." Swivelling, he took a step down the moonlit path.

Flint shot me a furtive look. I returned it.

"I'm coming to the meeting," I blurted.

Doc stopped. Turned. Looked at me.

"I know you're fond of Jayden, Nettle," he said. "But this is a meeting for the leadership team, and last time I checked, you weren't in it."

I swallowed. "No," I said. "But I need to be there anyway."

Doc raised an eyebrow. "Is that so?"

"Yes," I said, projecting more confidence than I felt. "To answer some questions that will inevitably come up."

Doc cocked his head. "What sort of questions?"

Chapter 22

Jayden

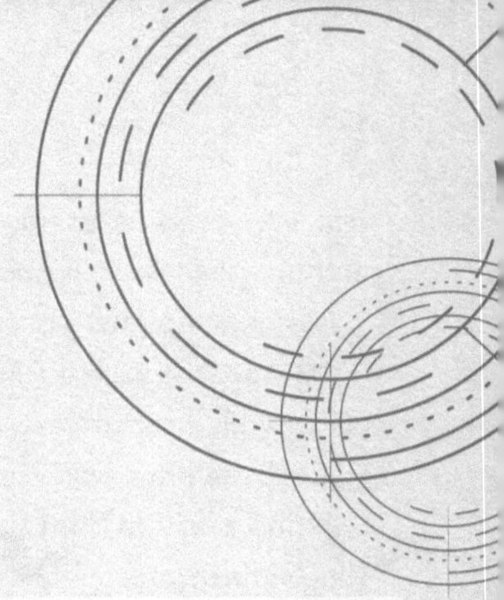

I MOVED MY GAZE from one silent face to another, panic building.

"What's wrong?" I asked at last. "We'll have the advantage of surprise, and I for one don't want to wait till we're surrounded to fight back."

Doc Aspen let out a heavy sigh. "We can't fight back, Jayden."

I stilled. Blinked. "What do you mean? Of course we can. We have to!"

"It would be a suicide mission," Doc said. "But we've already begun developing other shielded areas. We'll just have to relocate as much as we can. Keep our heads down."

"You don't think they'll see us?" I almost shouted. "By tomorrow, there'll be advance teams posted throughout this entire sector."

Doc pursed his lips, considering. "Then we'll have to surrender," he said.

Surrender? What did he mean—surrender?

"No," I said. "We can't surrender. Tun'll kill you for spite, and punish the rest of us with a life of virtual slavery underground."

"And you think it will be better if we go up against him and lose?"

"You're assuming we'll lose."

Doc Aspen shook his head. "Of course we'll lose. And if we resist, everything will be lost. Everything. The thousands of lives we hoped to save will be lost when the elite of Central abandon ship—as they will. The people of the colony are not equipped to survive, and the number of dead-zones *will* keep increasing, regardless of what Central wants to believe. The knowledge we have here"—he pointed to his head—"and here"—he pulsed his spread hands—"is irreplaceable. We must *live*, Jayden, even as slaves, to prevent something far worse. Otherwise, all we've accomplished will have been for nothing."

My chest hollowed out. No. No. They couldn't just give up.

"But we can keep the Masu safe," Doc continued, "at least for a time. We can tell them to leave, fly to safety, hide."

I still couldn't believe what I was hearing. "The colony commander will find a way to hunt them down," I said. "Now that he's convinced they're the problem, he won't give up. So we can't give up either."

"I really don't see that we have any other choice, Jayden," Doc Aspen said with another heavy sigh. "Masu can disable electronics, but they can do nothing against conventional small arms. You did well to get back here and warn us, but I'm afraid there's nothing more we can do. My brother-in-law will get his way for now, but when things inevitably start failing, at least we will have the skills to save those left behind."

Anger balled in my stomach. No! I did not risk getting killed just to hear them give up!

"Get some rest, everyone," Doc Aspen said, rising from his chair. "There'll be a lot to do tomorrow. Thank you for your efforts, Jayden."

This couldn't be happening. I'd come all this way and now...

I watched them begin to file out.

Something drained out of me, too. Was this it then? Should I just take their thanks, assume they knew what was best and go along with it? I'd be branded a traitor back in the colony; lose everything I just gained and for what? Nothing! Worse, I'd lose this place, and the secret hope it had given me, the wonder of connectedness, my senses brought to life...

I glanced over to where Nettle sat, her face a mask of horror. Suddenly unfreezing, she darted her eyes around like a cornered animal, trying to catch sight of something, anything, that could help her escape. Mine were the only eyes that met hers, but I'd already tried my best and failed.

Dammit! If I let them give in, I'd consign the woman I loved to a life of injustice and slavery beneath the hateful gaze of the regime she so despised. I couldn't do that.

And I was pretty sure Shana didn't endanger herself just to see that happen either.

I didn't get it. I just didn't get it. We had a decent chance! When the Masu set off every single damned node around Central Spire, we would have leverage; a negotiating position.

Half the leaders of the valley had already left when, after heaving increasingly heavy breaths, I yelled, "Stop!"

Faces turned towards me, and my shoulders rose and sank a few more times. "Stop," I repeated more quietly. "We can *do* this. We just have to strike before Tun does."

Doc Aspen shook his head sorrowfully. "Jayden, that's not our way, and besides, we have nothing to strike *with*."

"We have the Masu," I said, taking a step forward.

Doc Aspen's face hardened. "I am not going to ask the Masu to fight their way through small arms fire to rip out throats and disembowel people, Jayden! We set up this place so that the colony would *survive*! Not to destroy—"

"Wait," I interrupted him. "You think *that's* what I'm talking about? Tooth and claw?"

Doc looked confused. "That's... *not*... what you're talking about?"

"No!" I bellowed. "I'm talking about *disabling* Central, not some guerrilla raid. There are nodes all around the city, inside it. Five hundred Masu could shut Central Spire down with coordinated EMPs. Then Tun will *have* to listen."

Puzzled faces studied me. "Nodes?"

I blinked, just as puzzled. "Yeah, nodes. Those circular patches all over the ground that are the origin points of EMPs. Surely you've seen them when you were riding Masu, they're just like the electromagnetic auras surrounding each creature except..."

Blank stares regarded me.

"You've never seen them?" I asked. "Or the auras either?"

Heads shook, and it occurred to me that I'd never mentioned seeing them to either Flint or Nettle. I'd just assumed it was a result of the mind-link and was the same for everyone.

And it hadn't really seemed important to bring up when Flint's recovery and my impending return to the colony burdened my last days here.

"Tell us more about these nodes and auras, Jayden," Doc Aspen said, returning to the room and taking his seat. "Though the final decision will rest with the Masu."

Relief flooded me. "Well, I'm pretty sure the Masu can set them off at will..."

Chapter 23

Jayden

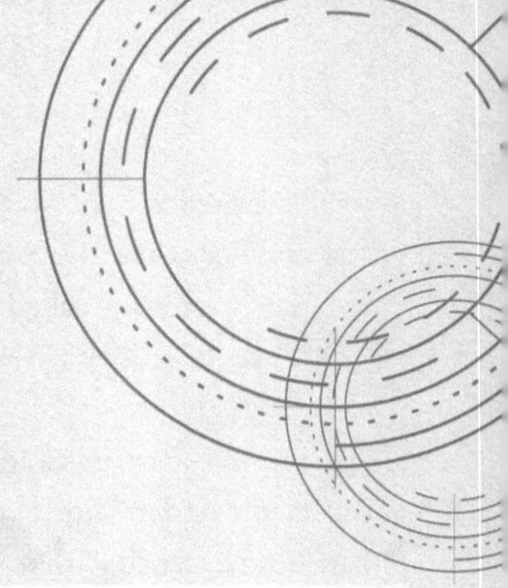

J UST BEFORE WE ENTERED the Masu den, hope and dread competing for supremacy inside me, I stopped Nettle with a hand on her arm. She turned around. "Whatever happens today, know that I don't regret it," I said, taking her hand in mine.

"I hope we both live to hear you say that again," she replied.

I pressed my lips into a line. "Me too."

I held her dark eyes with mine and stepped closer.

She moved closer too. "I'm so glad I didn't kill you," she said.

The urge to kiss her was almost overwhelming. Everything had conspired against this moment. "I'm so glad you didn't either," I said. "Sending me to look for you was the best mistake Central ever made." My voice grew a little husky, and the hand that wasn't clasping hers moved to cup her jaw.

She pressed into me, her hand sliding around my waist and up the centre of my back.

Pleasure curled through my stomach...

I lifted her face to mine...

She pulled back a little. "Wait, I thought you crashed by accident?"

Oh crap, why did I say that? And why hadn't I told Nettle the truth before I left?

"I... I did," I said, trying to recover. "I meant *finding you* was the best thing that ever happened to me. I..." I took a breath, then released it. "I love you, Nettle." It didn't matter how I got here. All that mattered was saving this place so we could be together in safety and freedom. I released her hand and held her waist instead. "I love you."

She sucked in her lower lip, then relaxed her body into mine.

I tilted my head and leaned in... at last...

"Hey lovebirds," called Flint. "Time to fly."

My eyes flew open before our lips even brushed, and the moment was lost.

Shuffling apart awkwardly, we turned to face a grinning Flint holding out two wooden shot glasses. Sighing, I took the miyu shot from his hand and downed it, the almost instant connection with Shana meaning I didn't even break stride. But I did give Nettle's hand another squeeze.

Two-hundred valley dwellers were mounted or saddling Masu. Another three-hundred riderless Masu milled about on the hillside or circled above. The majestic beasts had agreed the 'attack' was worth the risk for the chance to negotiate the cessation of hostilities. It was the next step in teaching us human cubs to live in harmony with their world. They'd wanted to from the moment we'd first arrived here but had understood caution was necessary, which was why they hadn't approached any humans until Doc's small group of rebels began to make secret caches away from the colony, or so Doc informed me.

But today, in a kind of territorial display, they would need to show they were a force to be reckoned with—albeit a restrained one. Far more restrained than untamed humans.

The plan was simple. Fly in low, set off strategic nodes, then get up out of small arms range. With Central disabled, some kind of parley could be attempted—I hoped. At the very least, the move would buy us enough time to relocate.

I found Shana, laid my head against the fur of her chest, and stroked her. I had a feeling it was more for my benefit than hers, but I could feel a rumbly purr beneath my cheek anyway. *You be careful*, I said. *I know you won't hurt them, but many of them will want to hurt you.*

Since Central roughly knew where the valley was, there was no point trying to hide our origin, so we took the direct route, in squadrons of about ten. I headed up the vanguard of mine with Flint and Nettle. The leadership had divided themselves up amongst the squadrons, and Doc

Aspen was with us too. Our designated role was to engage in negotiations.

As the nearest checkpoint tower came into view, the various squadrons peeled into two main groups to surround the colony before criss-crossing it. A flare of intense azure light with pops of violet and white, invisible to all but me and the Masu I guessed, consumed the nearest tower—just enough to fry the comms. Yelling ensued, but no gunfire—yet. There was too much confusion. We pressed on towards the city.

A tone rippled through me, and I saw selected nodes arc up as the Masu set them off. In a virtually silent attack, we swept through the city to Central Spire and dimmed the inner circle in our wake. Machines stopped. Lights went off. Tech crackled and buzzed into muteness. Then we were ascending to the heights, a great circling mass far above the startled population, still sparse at this hour.

Phase One: complete.

Shots *were* fired now, but too late. If one hit, it would be pure luck. So far, so good.

As alarms in the outer city sounded, the colony population began to emerge and gather in the squares and on the air-bridges, staring into the sky and pointing at us. With my senses linked to Shana's, I could see them clearly, but had no idea if Sarah or my parents were among them. It was early. They were probably still in the apartment wondering why no sim-coffee was coming.

The distinctive sound of 'thopter rotors coming up to speed reached my ears. Damn. Their extra shielding must have protected them. We'd need a more concentrated, close-range burst to get around that. If those 'thopters got into the air...

We have to disable them before they get out of the hangar, I communicated to Shana, and she dispersed the image of my plan to our squadron. Almost instantly, like a flock of birds all moving in uncanny unison, the ten of us were diving into the military quarter accompanied by the rattle of gunfire.

All ten Masu must have set off surges, and soon the 'thopters were thumping back down onto the hangar deck. A few of the more unfortunate ones landed on their sides or crashed to ground level twenty feet below. Major Reynolds ran out yelling expletives, and one of the Masu in my squadron took fire from the hangar guards. I had to do something quickly.

"Hold your fire!" I yelled, my voice somehow amplified beyond what was humanly possible—yet another strange manifestation of Masu abilities—"Unless you want every circuit in this place fried to a crisp!" It was a semi-bluff. The nodes probably needed to recharge, but we'd be back in control if the unit believed me.

Shana perched on a protected rooftop nearby, the bullets coming from below mainly shattering glass. The remainder of the squadron spread themselves around the other adjacent rooftops and the arch of the hangar. Another two squadrons had descended behind us, and were covering every other rooftop access point in the vicinity. From somewhere close, I heard a scream, and a sniper plummeted to the ground. On a rooftop across from me, a rifle had been seized and the gunman corralled into a corner. The shooting petered out. Still, I stared at Major Reynolds, his eyes burning with anger, until I saw him give the order to stand down.

"Captain Seymour!" the voice of Commander Tun bellowed through a megaphone.

I followed the sound to an air-bridge between the south and east Crystal Towers, and horror filled my eyes. Handcuffs held Sarah and my parents, and a squad of soldiers held guns to their heads.

"I figured you might come by with your kitties today, so I invited your family over to my place. Lucky they lived in the tower next door."

A ball of lead dropped into my stomach, and my heart clenched as I froze.

No. Our plans for neutral and rational negotiations were now just wreckage on the street. Tun had come prepared for a fight. Moreover, he'd executed his own son and daughter-in-law. He wouldn't hesitate to kill an upstart family from Wormsville.

"We came here to talk, Avery," Doc Aspen projected across the void, just as I had. "Not to massacre."

Commander Tun raised an eyebrow. "That so, Michael? Well, why don't you come over here and talk then?" It sounded more like a threat than an invitation.

Despite that, Doc gave us a nod, and I shook myself out of my trance. Shana flew me over to the air-bridge with the rest of our squadron, my mind still too much of a mess to give a coherent instruction. Six of us, including Flint, Nettle and Doc, alighted about thirty yards from where the colony commander stood, a little offset because of the curve, and the rest took up stations on the buildings nearby to give us cover.

Doc Aspen dismounted, and from my perch on Shana, I met Sarah's accusatory eyes. The aura around her screamed terrified fury, as did that around my parents, but Tun's aura was cool and green.

"Release Jayden's family," Doc Aspen said.

Tun smiled unpleasantly. "You just swooped in here and shut down half my city. Do you really expect me to give up the only card I have? I thought you more intelligent than that, Michael. I guess living in the wilderness took the edge off that once-sharp mind of yours."

Doc Aspen's face hardened. "What do you want, Avery?"

Tun spread his arms in an expansive gesture. "Same as always, Michael—growth and prosperity. To harness the assets in this land of opportunity and rise. Create a grand order, a great clockwork meshing of gears so all will—"

"Ensure that you, at least, have everything you could possibly want." Doc Aspen pursed his lips and gave a short, sharp nod. "Same as always."

A flicker of annoyance passed across Tun's face. "Careful, Michael."

"You were about to exterminate a native species for the sake of 'growth and prosperity'," Doc Aspen retorted. "And ruin our only *real* chance to live here in the process."

Tun snarled. "What is it that *you* want, then?"

Doc Aspen sighed. "Same as always. To seize this new opportunity, this second chance, and use the knowledge we've gained as a species to live in *harmony* with this world instead of destroying it. To provide a *real* future for the next generation."

Tun cocked an eyebrow. "Such as them?" He flicked his gaze at Flint and Nettle, and his other eyebrow joined the first in surprise.

"Mia? Lucas?"

I looked at Nettle. Flint also seemed confused.

"We're not called that anymore, *Grandfather*," she spat.

My lips parted in shock, though the pieces all fell together now.

Commander Tun recovered more quickly than me, and unexpectedly turned his eyes to lock onto mine. "Well done, Captain Seymour," he said in his now-smooth voice. "The final part of your mission is officially accomplished."

Nettle spun to regard me; narrowed her eyes. "What mission? What's he talking about?"

My heart lurched, my slip of the tongue from earlier coming back to haunt me. Tun would paint me as a double agent—and it was close enough to the truth to be believable.

The colony commander feigned surprise. "Oh, you didn't know?" he said. "The whole reason Captain Seymour crashed in the first place was because he was after reward money. And he got it too. What did you do with it, Seymour? Did you tell them?"

I looked at the colony commander with hatred in my eyes.

"Jayden?" Doc Aspen's eyes were troubled.

Dammit! Why was I such an *idiot*? I should have told them the truth ages ago! What part of my stupid brain had possessed me to think it didn't matter anymore because my heart had changed sides? They didn't know that! And now Tun would exploit my past weakness, making things sound much worse than they were.

Well, I would own it. I wouldn't let him turn me into a weapon.

"I bought my family a nice apartment and better jobs," I said through gritted teeth. "Which hardly seems to matter now, since they've got *guns* to their heads."

"Oh, that," said Commander Tun, waving the soldiers off. "They played along very nicely. As did you, Captain Seymour. Most convincing."

Nettle, Flint and Doc Aspen were all staring at me.

And Tun still had the upper hand. I was losing control.

"He's lying," I said, beginning to sweat. "Yes, originally, I planned to escape from the valley to get the reward, but by the time I got back here, I didn't care about it anymore. That's why I came back to warn you."

"You can drop the act now, Captain Seymour," Commander Tun said. "Don't worry, you'll still be paid your bonus."

How smoothly the venom rolled off this man's tongue.

And why were we talking about me anyway?

"What bonus!" I exploded. "There *is* no bonus! I risked my life getting out of here last night!"

"It had to look like that, certainly."

Rage surged through me, widening my eyes in a murderous glare and curling my lip into a snarl. "You snake. You lying, cowardly, dirty *snake*!"

Shana took a step forward in unity with my desire to kill him, her protective instincts aroused.

"We'll swap," Commander Tun said. "My family for yours, just like we agreed."

"We agreed on nothing!"

Every part of me felt tight. My jaw, my chest and arms, my stomach. I rounded on Doc Aspen. "Ask Shana," I said. "She'll tell you the truth."

I turned back to Tun. "You can't win this. I didn't tell you even *half* of what Masu can do."

What had even happened? He and Doc were just supposed to talk! Come to a peaceful compromise! But Tun was determined to get them to turn on me... undermine these negotiations with lies and distractions...

A sudden dread overcame me.

... or buy time.

Tun looked past us for just a second, and triumph flared in his aura.

"But you did tell me they weren't impervious to bullets," he said.

Sensing my alarm, Shana sprang into the air a microsecond before he gave his order.

"Shoot them."

Chapter 24
Nettle

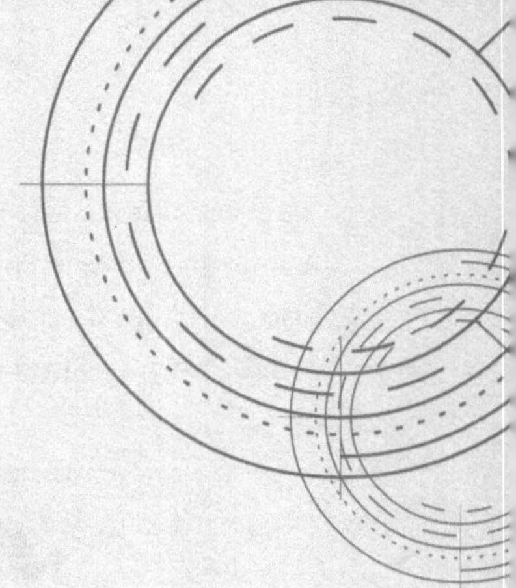

Timu dove from the air-bridge in unity with the other Masu as bullets sprayed across the place we'd been only seconds before.

It was a trap. This whole thing had been a trap.

Swirling underneath the air-bridge, bullets and screams following me, I rounded one of the towers and climbed, my chest tight and my eyes hot with betrayal.

Masu whooshed everywhere, the roars of pain echoing off the buildings indicating that at least some of them had taken fire. I glanced back to check on the squad, and my breath stopped.

Doc and his mount lay on the air-bridge below, sprays of red staining the concrete around them.

My insides hollowed out and my body froze in horror, gasps all I could manage.

No...

Doc Aspen was dead.

The man who'd rescued and raised Flint and me, and guided all of us in our fledgling years in the valley. The man who calmed and mediated, and held us together every time we almost fell apart. The man whose indestructible compassion had put the rest of us to shame.

Dead.

At the hands of Tun.

Just like my parents.

Except this time he'd had help.

Jayden.

Gritting my teeth in a snarl, I searched the sky for the traitor, furious that he'd seduced me into thinking he really cared.

Furious that I'd fallen for his act.

Furious that his double-dealing had even managed to deceive Shana.

From below me, Timu rumbled in disagreement. He hadn't deceived Shana.

He let slip this morning that he'd been sent *to us, Timu.* My mental voice was hard as steel. *He tried to cover it up, but he was lying through his teeth. To think I almost let him kiss me. To think I actually* wanted *to kiss that traitorous piece of Central filth.*

With that, I finally let out the scream of rage that had been trapped inside me.

Through our connection, I felt Timu grieve, but his anger didn't have the same quality as mine. There was no animosity towards Jayden. His was singularly directed against Tun.

Why are you defending him? I thundered. And why hadn't I slit Jayden's throat when I had the chance? None of this would have happened if I had. None of it! I let out another cry of rage wrapped in guilt—for in my headstrong stupidity, I had given that mole the means to betray us.

Hating myself, and hating Jayden, I scrubbed one forearm across my streaming eyes as we continued to climb.

Damn him!

Up ahead, I finally spied Shana just as she crested a tower to land on its roof.

I clenched my teeth. Timu sent reassurance.

How could two Masu trust him?

The truth. I would choke it out of him if I had to.

In unity with my desire, Timu banked and rode a thermal upwards.

Chapter 25

Jayden

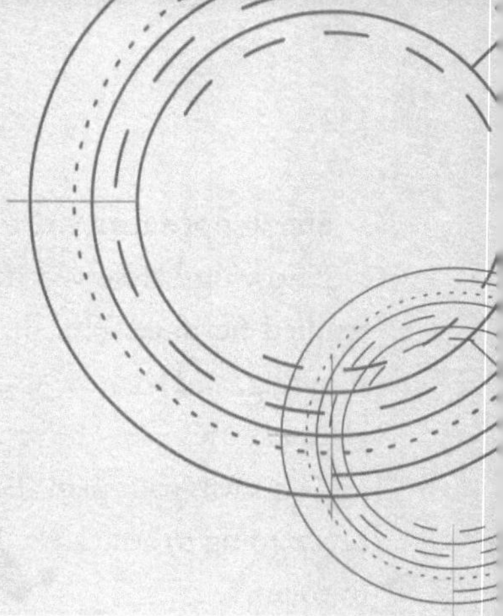

Sarah's screams followed me as I climbed out of rifle range. Doc and his Masu had been hit, and my roar of outrage joined her piercing shrieks of terror.

Everything inside me wanted Shana to dive back down and tear Commander Tun to pieces—but she didn't listen. Instead, she took me to the top of the East Tower, where those of us who remained were regrouping at a safe height. As soon as she came to rest, I tumbled from her back, barely able to breathe.

No, no. Doc Aspen—dead. It was impossible. Impossible... Dropping to my knees, I let out a guttural cry so loud Tun could probably hear it.

I didn't care.

Tears streaming down my face, I crawled to the edge of the tower's flat roof and looked over the edge. Splashes of red stained the deck of the air-bridge around the bodies of Doc and his Masu, the soldiers who'd emerged from behind us prodding at them with rifle barrels to make sure they were really dead. Sickened, I turned away.

Flint, similarly tear-streaked, shambled over to me. Neither of us knew what to say to the other. We just stared for a while, shocked and hurting, then Flint grabbed me and pulled me into a hug. My tears flowed anew.

As bursts of fire continued to sound from below, the others on the rooftop also stumbled over to join us. We became a great mesh of shaking bodies all leaning on one another, mourning Doc and all he stood for, and wondering what the hell we were supposed to do now.

Eventually we peeled away from each other, and I found myself looking at Nettle. Betrayal was in her eyes.

She stepped forward and slapped me.

Knowing I deserved it, I placed my hand on the stinging cheek and studied her face. Her lip was curled in a snarl, the white of her teeth showing, and shallow snorts of breath burst from her nostrils. Her eyes glared at me.

"This was your plan all along, wasn't it? To lure us all here. Central was *never* going to attack us. They didn't need to. They knew you'd bring us to them."

"No," I said, holding my hands palms out. "It wasn't like that at all, but I bet that cretin Tun was hoping I would." That's why I'd been invited to the briefing.

Nettle ignored me. "Did he send you specifically to find Flint and me?"

I shook my head. "No. That was a complete lie."

Her eyes remained hard and her mouth pinched. "This morning you said being sent to look for us was the best mistake Central ever made. How do you explain *that*?"

I slumped. Me and my stupid mouth. "That was referring to the first mission—the one that offered a reward for the location of your base. It was nothing to do with you personally."

Her glare remained unchanged. "You said you were flying a routine mission then."

I let out a breath, my insides completely caving. "I lied," I said, hating myself. "I'd just crashed and almost had my throat cut. I was... scared."

At last Nettle's expression changed—slightly. Her mouth remained a thin line, but her brows at least came back to neutral. She seemed to be considering something.

"Why didn't you tell me about the reward?"

I looked down, shame burning me. "I wanted to. I almost did... but I was too big a coward. I'm sorry."

A thick silence hung between us, then: "Were you telling the truth just now? On the air-bridge?"

Her stormy eyes pierced mine when I looked up. "Yes," I said, holding them desperately. "Every word. I hated living in that stinking tower. Every single day, I wanted to be back with you in the valley. Here, look"—I reached into an inner pocket and pulled out my wooden spoon—"I kept this with me all the time, to remind me of you, and the life I had to leave behind just as I decided it was what I wanted more than anything."

She took it from my hand, turned it over in hers.

"I wouldn't even let a domesti-bot touch it."

Grinding my teeth, I looked over my shoulder towards the place where my family was still held captive. "But now it's all for nothing anyway. That bastard Tun is holding my family for ransom. I lose no matter which way I jump."

Nettle handed the spoon back to me. "I... believe you," she said, face troubled, "but this plan of yours has failed, and now we're facing the retaliation of a madman."

There was another silence.

"The Masu can still leave," Flint said after a moment, raising his eyes to the many circling high overhead. "We won't forget the skills we learnt. The forge and the other things we made will remain. No matter how powerful he is, Tun can't hold back the encroaching tide of tech failure. Soon everyone'll beg us for the knowledge we have."

"I don't know," said Nettle, shaking her head. "I think our 'grandfather' is the type to take the entire ship down with him. And I'd rather die than live here as a prisoner—a nothing—with a threat hanging over my head *every single day*."

I shifted. She was right, and I couldn't do it to her. It would kill her to live under the man and regime that executed her parents and now Doc.

Flint heaved a breath. "So, whadda we do then?"

Dead silence.

"I... I could offer myself in exchange," I said. "Maybe... maybe the rest of you could escape. Go further away. Start again..."

Nettle's brow pinched. "Jayden—"

"I've lived here before. I can do it again." I held myself rigid, gritting my teeth. "You... you can't. I won't let you." I began walking towards the edge of the tower roof.

Nettle grabbed my sleeve. "Jayden, no—"

Tun's megaphone crackled into life. "Shame about what happened down here. Even more of a shame if your family joined *Doc* and his kitty, Captain Seymour. You've got two minutes to convince your friends to surrender their rebel asses. Generous, I'd say, given your surprise attack this morning."

I clenched my teeth. I hated this man to the core of my being. First, he'd killed Flint and Nettle's parents—one of whom was his own *child*—as a deterrent to the rest of us. Then, indifferent, he'd ground us all into the dust so that he and his inner circle could live in luxury. He'd tricked good pilots into a suicide mission, and cared about his bottom line more than long-term survival. Now he threatened all I loved: my blood family who I'd risked everything to give a better life to, and my new family, who'd risked everything to welcome me among them.

But if I surrendered myself, Nettle might be able to escape, and the Masu, at least, could go free. This was their planet. It was just a shame their experiment with us humans had failed.

Tugging my arm out of Nettle's grasp, I finished my walk to the edge and stared down at Tun. "Take me instead."

Tun cocked his head, then outright laughed. "What makes you think I want a worm like you, Seymour?"

The blood drained from me. The only other option I'd thought of had just evaporated in Tun's derogatory laughter.

Now, it was back to two impossible choices, for if we fought, my family would die. If we surrendered, we may as well all be dead.

And I had about a minute and half to decide which it would be.

Shana nudged me, rubbing her great head against my arm. Letting me know she was here for me. Here for us.

Wait...

I remembered the strange, blank looks of the checkpoint guards right before they'd let my escorts go. That... that had been Shana. The shooting had petered out *before* Major Reynolds had given the stand-down command too...

I whipped around to Flint. "Flint," I said, "when I asked how you tamed the Masu, you told me you didn't, that they tamed you, yes?"

Flint nodded slowly. "Yes..."

"How?" I asked, growing excited now. "How did it happen?"

"They kind of reached out with an embrace of musical light... peace. A... vision? Awareness? It was like we saw how things could be if we just... let go of our fear? Something like that? I don't quite remember."

My breaths came fast. "Do you think they could do it again? Here? Now?"

Flint caught onto my meaning, and his face broke into a smile. "Absolutely they could. No miyu necessary."

I turned to Nettle. "What do you think?"

Nettle bit her lip. "It's a big change in plan... all these people."

I grasped her hands. "They're just as much Tun's victims as we are."

She screwed up her forehead, closed her eyes, exhaled. Finally, she nodded. "You're right."

I breathed a sigh of relief, hope returning. "Then let's ask the Masu."

Shana understood immediately, and warm, rumbly purring answered me. Through the implicit connection she shared with the others, I learnt they felt the same way. There was a unified sense that it was time for this.

And that's when I realised what we were actually attempting. If we succeeded, it wouldn't just be for today. A tentative peace requiring vigilance to maintain. No. We would reunite the people. Achieve Doc's dream. The Masu dream.

And that's why the Masu wouldn't force anyone. Wouldn't break anyone. But Shana seemed to think they wouldn't need to. That most of the minds here were like mine. Different.

I had no idea what she meant by that, but it reassured me.

Ok then. The squad with Tun, will you tame them first? I asked. *Not Tun though. Leave him to me.* Even if Shana was confident about the others, Tun's mind would certainly break if she tried to connect. I just hoped he'd see sense and surrender.

From the sky above, hundreds of Masu descended, risking fire to alight on the tops of the towers, factories and domes. A different kind of energy went out from them, and even though a few got hit, the shooting slowed, then stopped. Through Shana, I felt the peaceful, harmonising tones of a million tuning forks radiate towards the soldiers—that gentle embrace of light and sound that had 'caught' me when I first spun out of control in the void opened by the miyu. I sensed shock, resistance, much like I had felt initially, and then, as they heard their names spoken—the vibration of *their* essence within the whole—the release of knowing that where they were was the safest place in the world.

"Time's up, Captain," Tun called over his megaphone, "and given you've called in the kitties, I can guess you're officially a rebel now. So very sorry Mr. and Mrs. Seymour, Sarah, but I can't imagine how you'd live knowing you raised a traitor anyhow."

He paused.

"Shoot them."

Chapter 26

Jayden

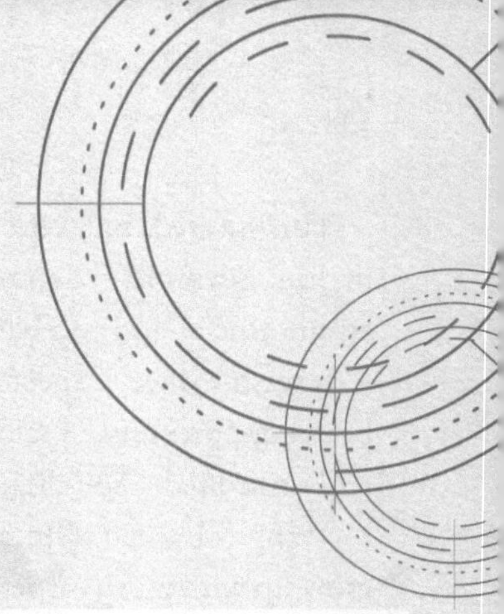

MY INSIDES KNOTTED. WOULD it work?

From the edge of the building, I saw the soldiers hesitate, then the sergeant shook his head. "This... this isn't right, sir."

Tun clenched his jaw. "You questioning my orders, Sergeant?"

The sergeant looked uncomfortable a moment, then put his shoulders back. "Yes, sir, I am." He turned to his squad. "Take them to safety while we work this out."

Looking relieved to have orders to follow, the others slung their rifles, but before they could do much more than that, Tun exploded.

"Either you shoot them, or I'll shoot them myself!" Throwing the megaphone at the sergeant, he kicked the rifle out of his hands and drew his own sidearm, pointing it straight at Sarah.

Reacting fast, the sergeant knocked the weapon off-course, the crack of the bullet sending a puff of concrete dust into the air at Sarah's feet. She screamed.

Everything inside me screamed with her, then firmed. *Ok Shana, time to tame Tun.*

But the colony commander's conversion would be up to me, not her.

After I jumped on Shana's back, we glided down to the air-bridge, then, flaring, Shana landed with a scrape of claws on concrete just as the squad was hustling my family into the South Tower.

"You've lost, Commander." Almost throwing myself out of the saddle, I swiped up the sergeant's rifle and strode towards the wrestling pair. "Face it." It was just the four of us on the air-bridge now, the ambush squadron having been dismissed sometime earlier.

Tun sneered, but kept his grip on the handgun. "I'm disappointed in you, Seymour," he said. "I offered you a golden opportunity for advancement, and you blew it."

It wasn't what I expected him to say, but I had my answer. "I found a better opportunity," I said. "And now I offer it to you. Join us."

Tun scoffed. "You disgust me, Seymour."

"Why?" I asked. "Because I'm from Wormsville? Because I didn't grow up with plush carpet under my feet and real food to eat and toadies who would jump to do my will?"

Tun's lip curled, and he made another attempt to wrench the weapon out of the sergeant's grip. "The world is full of two types of people, Seymour: the ones who have those things, and the ones who want them."

"You're wrong," I said, adjusting my grip on the rifle a little. "There's a third kind of person: those who are content with what they have."

"Naïve fairy tales, Seymour." A derisory shake of his head accompanied Tun's mocking laughter. With a sneer, he released the gun in a supreme show of arrogance, almost pushing it into the sergeant's hands before folding his arms across his massive chest. "There's no prosperity without growth, and there's no growth without competition. Humans need people at the top. We're built like this. Survival of the fittest. I run this place so that talented and ambitious people like you will succeed; rise to the top like cream. You don't disgust me because you're from Wormsville. You disgust me because you're sentimental."

His words were meant to deflate me, but they had the opposite effect. "Better to be sentimental than short-sighted."

Again, Tun laughed. "Short-sighted. That's a good one. Have you *really* thought long-term? You and your rebels might be united now because you have me as your common enemy, but soon things will start falling apart and you'll find yourselves scrambling for power. The strongest will win. It's the way of nature. You can't fight it."

He moved his hands to his hips and eyed me with disdain.

I kept my stare intent. "The Masu could show you something different."

"What? These *creatures*?" He threw a scathing look and hand at Shana. "You think a *beast* knows how the world works?"

"They know how *this* world works."

"You're delusional. You're all delusional." This time the sergeant also came under his contemptuous regard.

"Not delusional. We've just seen more. You've only seen what you've lived—an untouchable, privileged life. A life you were conditioned to believe you deserved. But dignity is not a limited commodity. Neither is opportunity. The strong can make sure there's enough. Sacrifice. The Masu are the apex predator on this planet, yet they don't exploit. Because they're not afraid." I smiled up at Shana, then stroked her on the neck.

Tun snarled. "You calling me a coward?"

I hadn't actually thought of that, but as Tun denied it, I realised it was true. He was afraid. Every decision he made had its roots in fear.

I locked eyes with him. "You said it, not me."

The snarl morphed into a sneer. "You wouldn't be half so brave without that rifle in your hands and that monster at your back. Face it, Captain, we're not so different. We both know the strong win. And right now, you think you're stronger than me."

The words hit me in the gut. He was right.

I glanced at the rifle I held relaxed at my hip. Symbol of power. Dominance. I'd picked it up by instinct, to protect myself, to uphold my right to be heard.

Because in my head I was still a worm.

All my life, I had bought into the idea that only those aboveground had value in this colony, and I needed to claw my way out of the pit I'd been unfortunate enough to be born into. Despite everything, I hadn't let that idea go. I wanted security, freedom, and respect every bit as much as I ever did—and I wanted to defend my right to them.

Because I was still afraid.

Gritting my teeth, I tossed the weapon aside. "I don't need to be stronger than you. We don't need to fight."

One of Tun's eyebrows rose just a bit.

I took a pace towards his immense figure.

"Don't you want a relationship with your grandkids again? Your sister? Don't you want to know that your descendants will still be around a thousand years from now, because of a decision you made to work *with* this world instead of *against* it? Don't you want to know what it's like to not worry about proving your importance to everyone around you?"

Tun's smile was nasty. "It's not that simple. It's never that simple."

"It can be," I said, taking another pace forward. "I've lived it."

"With these *creatures*?" He gestured toward Shana in a derogatory manner, then took up his intimidating stance once more, casting a side-eye at the sergeant who still half-heartedly pointed the handgun in his direction.

"Yeah," I said, calm. "They're just enough creature to realise they don't need to prove themselves or be anything other than what they are. They're just enough creature to realise they are but *one* part of life, and that all have a place. All have value. They know how to take no more than they need, and to *want* no more than they need. These creatures have taught me how to be human."

At that, Tun cocked his head. After a moment, he relaxed a little.

His aura became muddied, and he looked at me, then Shana.

"We don't have to perpetuate the old system," I said. "On earth, we were more savage than animals. Here, perhaps we can actually be what we're capable of being. Integrate, instead of imposing ourselves. Be the colonised, instead of the colonisers for once. That's what Doc was working towards."

Tun stared a moment more, then looked at the concrete.

I extended a hand. "We can work together. What do you say?"

Tun slumped a little. "I say..." He let out a breath, then, lightning quick, wrested the gun out of the sergeant's hand and kicked him in the chest. The sergeant's head hit the railing with a thud and his body slid to the deck, his aura dulled.

Tun turned the weapon on me. "I say you're full of crap, Seymour, and I'm gonna enjoy proving you wrong. Your kitties may have brainwashed you, and brainwashed my men, but they're not going to brainwash me."

I lunged for the rifle as Tun's bullet shot past me, expecting at any moment that a second round would finish me off...

But the gun never fired.

Mystified, I looked up to see Tun frozen in place, his features slack.

And I felt peace.

Flooding me.

Not soft, fluffy peace.

Powerful peace.

A vibrational resonance that almost felt solid.

And I realised Shana had mind-locked with Tun.

My heart fell. *Shana, no, you said you didn't want to break anyone...*

I tried to stop her, interrupt her line of sight, tug on her. She shouldn't have to compromise herself. Shouldn't have to go against what she believed because I had failed. We had one shot at unification, and if I'd screwed up, it should be me paying, not her.

I glanced at Tun, frozen like a statue, then back at Shana. Maybe if I just had more time, I could get him to the point where she could try this; get him to take some miyu; *something*!

Shana... please...

All I got in response was an image of her protecting another set of cubs from that same giant striax python.

Tun was a predator, and she'd made her choice. Loss was a part of life, yes, but to stand by and not defend the weak went against her nature as much as taking revenge did.

Besides, they'd given him one chance to yield. This would be another.

I shifted my gaze from her back to Tun. Had I done enough? There was a look of wonder on his face as he stared at images unseen, blue light surrounding him.

A profound stillness—music felt rather than heard—hung over the entire area, almost like everything had been swept inside the same embrace of light Tun was now held in. There were no screams of panic from below, no running feet. Masu had descended en masse during our confrontation, and the people were mesmerised, just like I had been when I first saw the creatures.

In a sudden rush of air, startlingly loud in the thick quiet, Asha landed, and Flint stole up beside me.

"Is he...?"

"Shhh."

Tun was softening—I could see it. The arm holding the handgun lowered, and the commander's eyes turned shiny. A tear escaped from the corner of one. His mouth dropped open, and his fingers loosened. He was letting go of his fear.

Could Shana actually win him over? Could Tun truly be tamed?

The gun fell from his grasp...

... and hit the air-bridge with a metallic clunk.

The sound shattered the reverent silence... and Tun went rigid.

No... no...

His resistance, that same resistance I had felt to the sensation of falling, had kicked in.

But there would be no relaxing into Shana's embrace for him.

Within moments, Tun's features turned from soft to twisted, and he began shaking. The light surrounding him snapped to orange, his discordant frequency piercing the calm like a scream.

Now, instead of allowing it, he fought the vision Shana was giving him, and his opposition was as powerful as the EM wall surrounding the valley.

I balled my hands into fists. No. No! We'd lost. It was painful to watch.

"His mind's going to break any moment now," Flint whispered beside me, "just like Vine's. He's too in love with control."

Strangled shrieking escaped Tun's throat as he fell to his knees, then movement in my periphery ignited fear—more soldiers pouring onto the air-bridge.

"Flint?"

"It's ok," he said, eyes still fixed on Tun, "they're on our side now."

The sergeant, on his feet again, held up a palm to the soldiers and then beckoned them to approach slowly.

Now a seizure gripped the commander, and his body writhed on the concrete as he jerked and shuddered, no longer held in Shana's grip, but the prison he'd made for himself.

Beside me, Shana hung her head, then fixed her gaze on the sergeant. He nodded and stepped over to Tun, rolling the colony commander onto his side so he wouldn't do himself damage.

I felt gutted. Even though I'd tried, then Shana tried, it hadn't been enough. For a moment there, the realisation of a dream had been within reach. We'd been so close, so close. For a moment there, I had hoped that even someone as hard as Tun could understand how much more desirable it was to live synergistically with this planet... unite with it...

But no; we'd failed. *I'd* failed.

Swallowing, I looked away, let my forehead fall against Shana's chest, and tried to block out Tun's gurgling moans.

After I don't know how long, I felt Flint's hand on my shoulder.

"Jayden," he said, "it's ok."

My throat felt tight. "Maybe, but it could have been so much better."

"He was offered the chance to be part of the Balance, Jayden," Flint said, turning me towards him, "but he chose not to take it."

I screwed up my face in pain, covered it in one hand, squeezed. After another moment, I exhaled through my teeth. "You're right," I said. "You're right. It's just..."

"It doesn't feel like a victory."

"Yeah."

"But it is," said Flint. "Come look."

He guided me to the railing, and directed me to look at what was happening below. Masu were dotted along the roadways and in the plazas, sitting like huge sphinxes among the adults and children who came forward to touch them.

A half-hearted smile tried to make it onto my face, but couldn't quite push through the defeat. Not yet. Still, as I watched the scene unfold below, hope stirred. In this part of the city, people were flowing up out of the emergency exits, and as they stepped into the light, their shocked cries mostly turned to exclamations of wonder, or laughter. Some people, emanating fearful yellow light, hung back though, clinging to corners and grabbing at the clothing of those drawn forth in violet-shrouded awe. Like Tun, not all would embrace the gift the Masu offered, but it looked like enough would.

A half-smile, half-grimace turned the corners of my mouth. I made a semi-hopeful grunt, but when I turned to Flint, something over his shoulder caught my eye.

Sarah had tentatively stepped out onto the air-bridge.

Oh, crap... My family probably hated me. Would they even want to see me again after what I put them through?

Scanning the area, Sarah found me. Our eyes connected.

Radiating green, she beamed.

Both guilt and relief swept through me as I ran and embraced her.

"I'm so sorry," I said. "I almost got you guys killed!"

Sarah said nothing, but I could sense the tears squeezing out of her eyes as she crushed me. At length, we loosened our grip, and I became aware of others close by, as well as the wind of a Masu landing.

Sarah pushed away and stared at me.

At me, and around me.

"Jayden... what's happening?" she asked. "You're... you're glowing. Everyone's glowing."

I started. "You... you can see that?" Was it because she was my sister? No, wait... Shana had said lots of minds here were different... like mine. "The virus..." I breathed.

And almost everyone had had it to some degree...

I looked over my shoulder to where Tun still jerked on the ground.

Everyone but the elite of Central...

I turned back to Sarah and saw my parents approaching. My dad's arm was around my mother, and she gripped one of his hands. Her aura was muddied, and I couldn't tell if she was angry or still traumatised by what had just happened.

Maybe it was both.

Letting go of Sarah, I walked over to them. "I'm sorry," I said. "I never meant for you to get involved in this. I didn't know Tun would…"

"We all underestimated the colony commander," my father said. "Or perhaps overestimated him." He craned his neck to look at the man, who'd started moaning again. "But I guess he can't do any more harm now."

I glanced over my shoulder. "Let's hope not. But the damage he's already done is bad enough," I said. "All the activities of the colony, the oscillium mining especially, have been triggering the multiplication of the dead-zones, and he kept that knowledge secret. If we don't stop, they'll just keep popping up, and everything here will stop working."

My mother's eyes widened. "Everything?" she said.

"Yeah. But there's another way to live. That's what Doc and all the others wanted to create—a safe haven for everyone, so we weren't killing ourselves over scarce resources, and everyone had a chance at life."

"That's why you chose them over us," Sarah said.

I felt another stab of guilt, but realised there was more to it than that. "No. I chose them, so I could choose you *too*," I said. "It was never a competition."

Everyone was quiet, then my mother reached for my hand. "Thank you," she said. "And this time my hero doesn't get away without having a *proper* hug."

She pulled me towards her, and, grateful beyond telling, I gripped her tight. It was ok. It really was ok. But I needed to do things differently this time round. I wouldn't leave them in the dark.

When we released each other, I looked at them all seriously. "I want to take you to the valley today," I said. "You and as many as we can double on the Masu. Just pack a few things, and we'll get going in a couple of hours."

They nodded and returned to the tower, Sarah glancing over her shoulder one last time before disappearing inside.

Exhaling in relief, I looked around again. Now colonists and valley-dwellers were having conversations, and heaps of kids crowded around the Masu, their laughter and squeals of delight a welcome strangeness in this place of grey efficiency.

I may have lost the battle with Tun, but there was still a victory to celebrate today.

Allowing myself an almost-smile, I flinched when Nettle snuck up behind me and put her arm around my waist, and within seconds, the smile became real. Tingling spread throughout my chest and cascaded all the way down to my toes as I turned towards her. Her eyes were still glistening, but happiness was mixed in now. Wordlessly, I wrapped her in my arms and pulled her close, leaning in to press my lips onto hers.

We melted together, and heaven touched Osivirius.

Completely overcome, my chest hollowed, suddenly empty of breath as my eyes rolled pleasantly backwards. Air returned, shared with her in shallow bursts, though my stomach remained tight with both desire and release.

For a time, nothing else existed—just her soft lips on mine, her silky hair beneath my fingers, and the warm press of her body. Her floral scent filled my senses, somehow having survived the harrowing morning, and the only reason I broke away from her was a desperate need to see her face.

Her eyes, soft now, held mine, and her mouth curved. A breath escaped.

"Jayden," she whispered, "we did it."

My own breath released, and I felt the triumph at last—though couldn't accept the credit for it. "Not us," I disagreed. "The Masu."

Shana seemed to smile as she padded towards us both, and Flint nudged me in the ribs—which was very unfair of him, since I was still holding his sister and my sides were exposed.

"Hey lovebirds," he quipped. "Time to fly."

Chapter 27
Nettle

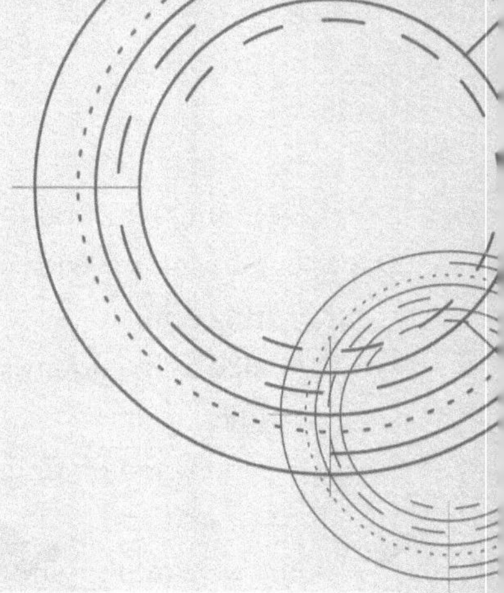

MY BROTHER'S TIMING WAS impeccable as always.

"Not so fast, Flint," Jayden said, breaking away from me. "We're taking some of them with us."

My chest tightened. "We're... what?"

Jayden, still with one hand relaxed around my waist, held my gaze. "I just told Sarah and my parents to gather some things together. I want to take as many as we can double back to the valley."

"That was never part of the plan," I said, panic rising. My valley. Invaded.

"I know it wasn't," Jayden said. "But neither was taming the entire population, or leaving them leaderless. We've got to show them what's possible. Teach them."

"Also feed them," Flint added, ever the kind-hearted medical student.

"But..."

"It'll be fine," Jayden reassured me. "There're good people in Wormsville. And Sarah's biodome crew will be perfect students."

Uneasiness pooled in my stomach. I pulled the inside of my lower lip between my teeth, then released it, though my brow remained pinched. "I guess..."

Jayden kissed me—swiftly this time—but trailed his fingers along my jawline as he smiled down at me. My insides fluttered despite myself.

"It'll be fine, trust me," he said again. "Hold the fort?"

I managed a nod, but my stomach roiled as I watched him and Flint stride toward Shana and Asha, laughing and bumping into each other in boyish camaraderie.

Left alone, I turned the other direction—and saw the colony commander sitting up with a vacant stare in his eyes, a crouching soldier supporting him.

The sick feeling in my stomach turned to lead.

A soldier.

My eyes darted around.

Lots of soldiers.

They were milling about, blocking my view of Doc and his Masu...

I swallowed.

The valley wouldn't be the same.

My life wouldn't be the same.

I turned away.

"Miss?"

I froze. The soldier who was with Tun was calling to me.

"Excuse me, miss?"

Drawing in a breath of courage, I turned around. "Yes, what is it?"

"I saw you, um, talking, to Captain Seymour," he said. "Do you have any idea what's going on? Someone needs to take charge here before people start asking questions. The population will be fine for a little while, but then they'll wanna know someone's got a plan. My guys can help."

My mouth went dry. Soldiers? Help?

"Uh, thanks," I said, then took a step towards the two of them, mostly because I thought I should. "We're gonna fly some people back to our base, teach them what's safe to eat, and other useful things. Probably fly some supplies back here."

The soldier nodded. "Ok then. So we should organise people back into their billets. Set up food and information stations. See what we can get back up and running."

Kind of in a daze, I watched as he called some others to him. He got one of them to take over supervising the commander—my grandfather, though I'd never thought of him as that—while he briefed the group. Each soldier nodded sharply as his assignment was issued, then jogged off to complete the task. The calm efficiency of it left me paradoxically in turmoil.

I'd spent most of my life hating this efficiency. This unquestioning obedience to orders. It was this very thing that had led to my parents being shoved, all bloodied, into a transport and later executed.

But these soldiers weren't heartless.

Any more than Jayden was heartless.

I moved my gaze to my grandfather. *He* was the heartless one. But it was hard to be angry at him when he had saliva dribbling out of the corner of his mouth.

Disgust and pity collided. Vied for supremacy. Could I forgive him? And could I learn to care for these people I'd hated all my life? Share with them what I'd worked so hard for?

That's what Doc had wanted to do.

The briefing ended, and the soldier walked over to me.

Fear returned, but he just held out his hand. "Sergeant McAllister," he said, "if you need to find me."

I looked at his hand, deciding whether or not it was safe, then haltingly extended my own. With a sharp inhalation, I grasped it and shook.

"Nettle," I said.

Chapter 28

Jayden

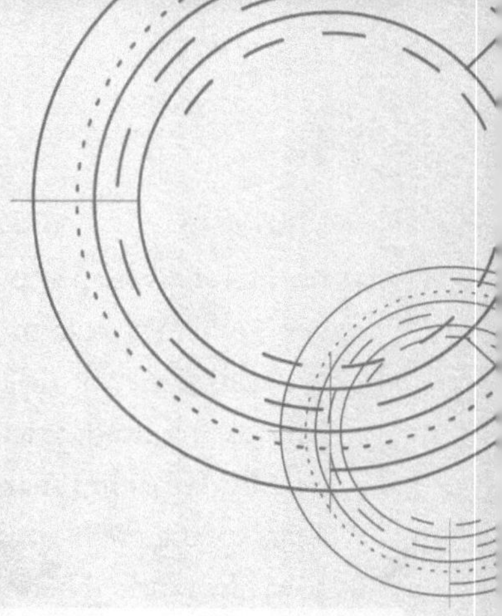

J UST SHY OF TWO hundred colonists hitched a ride to the valley, and I made sure I got as many willing denizens of Wormsville into that first group as possible. They were the powerhouse of the colony—and the ones who would make other valleys like this one come to life.

Sarah, with her biodome crew, would also catch on quickly. Her arms had gripped me like a vice when we'd first taken off, but now sat comfortably around my waist as I doubled her on Shana.

Her gasp as we crested the ridge gratified me, and I sensed some of the awe she felt as we lazily circled down to the ledge in front of the Masu den.

"It's beautiful."

It was. The waterfall sparkled as it tumbled down the mountainside and into the lake below, trees laden with fruit waved glossy green fronds, and faces full of relief and excitement smiled up at us from the cave mouths that dotted the valley wall.

I was so ready to touch down, then disappear somewhere private and crown this day of triumph with Nettle in my arms. There were plenty of others who would be much more skilled at organising meals and finding places for everyone to sleep. Tomorrow. Tomorrow I would face the crazy-amazing task I'd set myself: creating the world I wanted to live in.

We landed, and Shana made herself as flat as possible to give Sarah an easy dismount. More Masu swarmed in, eager faces on the ledge searching for their friends and loved ones. Not far away, Timu flared and touched his back feet to the stone. A moment later, his front paws dropped down, and Nettle and my mother slid off.

I grasped Sarah's hand and was just about to walk over to them when a grey-haired woman approached me. My face dropped. It was Lily, Doc Aspen's wife. She read my expression.

"Jayden? Is Aspen alright?"

I shook my head, grief rising up from the place I'd pushed it. "I'm sorry, Lily. He didn't make it. Commander Tun—" I couldn't go on.

Tears sprang to her eyes, and I let go of Sarah's hand to embrace Doc's widow. She crushed herself into my chest.

"He did us proud," I said, rubbing her back. "He was fearless."

I could feel her nodding against my chest. "He always was. I knew it would be his downfall one day. I just didn't want it to be *this* day."

I hugged her tight. "None of us did. He was the best of men." My own eyes glistened again at the memory of him being gunned down without mercy.

"What about Avery?" Lily asked, pushing away from me slightly.

Damn. Commander Tun was her brother.

"Alive, but deranged now. Worse than Vine. He refused to be tamed."

She closed her eyes. "His stubborn pride was always going to be *his* downfall. That, and his spitefulness."

I didn't know what to say.

Others who'd known Lily much longer than I came to offer condolences, and she was soon surrounded. I gratefully relinquished her to their care. Grabbing Sarah's hand again, I drew her away from the crowd and scanned for Nettle, but she and Flint were making their way over to Lily.

I suppressed my disappointment. It was perfectly understandable that the siblings would want to be with the woman who'd been their foster mother in her time of grief, like she'd been in theirs.

Standing there awkwardly, I waited for Nettle and Flint to find us. At last, I caught Flint's eye. The ledge was getting more and more crowded, so I motioned to them to follow us down to the herb gardens.

"So," said Flint after they arrived, "this is your sister?"

I looked at him a little weirdly. "Uh, yeah, this is Sarah," I said. "Sarah, these are my friends, Flint and Nettle."

"Hi," said Sarah. "I don't think I've ever heard those names before. They're nice. Kind of 'earthy'."

Flint smiled. "They're meant to be. And it's time *you* got a new name too, Jayden."

"What? Me?"

"Flint and I talked about it," Nettle said, "and because you're officially a rebel now, you need a rebel name."

"I'm dubbing you 'Miyu'," Flint said, "because you're a true son of Osivirius, and you brought us together, just like miyu opened the connection with the Masu."

Kind of stunned, I laughed. "Well, I guess it's better than 'gupi'."

"Or 'cactus'." Nettle smirked.

"Do I get a new name?" asked Sarah.

Flint got a glint in his eye. "I'm sure we can arrange that," he said, "but for now, how about a tour?" He extended his elbow to her like a gentleman of old, and, blushing a little, Sarah took it.

I watched them wander away, Flint smiling and gesturing while Sarah giggled. Letting out a contented sigh, glad to finally be alone with Nettle, I turned back to her.

My face fell.

She was fingering a plant, a sorrowful look on her face.

"Are you thinking about Doc?" I asked, moving to put a hand on her shoulder.

She shook her head. "I'm not ready for this, Jayden."

I stilled. "What are you not ready for?"

"This... this *change*," she said, turning melancholy eyes to mine. "I know it's the right thing to do, but it's still hard."

Oh.

So much for sweeping her into my arms and kissing her breathless. I dropped my hand.

"Maybe it won't be as bad as you think."

"Maybe it'll be worse," she countered, plucking a leaf and crushing it. "We left the colony wanting to create something special. Something integrated and egalitarian. Familial. Yes, there have been problems, but we all had the same fundamental goal and vision. We *wanted* to make it work."

She sighed and let the pieces of leaf fall to the ground. "None of these people have that background, Jayden," she said. "There'll be complaining, protests, leadership struggles. And believe it or not, they'll miss their synth mush."

My forehead knitted. I reached for her hand. "I came around."

"You were a single person, and you had *Flint* looking after you," she said with a slight eye-roll. After letting me hold her hand a moment, she spread her fingers to disengage and began walking through the garden.

I followed her. "But they've been touched by the Masu," I said, grasping for something to reassure her and restore her earlier happiness. "That... changes people. It's what finally changed me. And I think the Balance and whatever other forces control this world want it to happen. That virus that ripped through the colony? *It* changed us too."

Nettle had reached the end of the terrace, where a railing had been built. She leant against it on her elbows and gazed off into the distance. "I hope you're right," she said. "'Cos trusting that is the only thing stopping me from breaking down right now."

I watched a tear slide from her eye as she surveyed the valley that had been her safe haven for so long. The safe haven I'd invaded, then compromised, and now wanted to share with everyone.

I put my hand on her shoulder again, but couldn't quite look at her. I hadn't realised until this moment how much Nettle had sacrificed when she said 'yes' to asking the Masu to tame everyone, then 'yes' to flying colonists here.

And shame burned my insides.

"I shook hands with a soldier today," she said in a half-whisper, like she didn't quite believe it herself. "Sergeant McAllister. He offered to help organise things."

The way she said it—so small, so distant—stabbed at me, and I squeezed in on myself, stuffing down the guilt. But it was no use. With an ache, I realised the courage that would have taken. How hard it would have been.

And I had just left her to face it. Didn't even think about it.

I was such a jerk.

Letting my hand drop away, I crashed onto my own elbows and hung my head.

"I... I'm sorry, Nettle," I said. "I shouldn't have left you alone."

I stayed there for a while, hating myself, until I had to look up. Had to see.

Finally, Nettle looked at me. There was such hurt in her stormy eyes. I felt about three-inches tall.

But I forced myself to keep looking.

"And... and I shouldn't have sprung this plan on you. Presumed you'd be ok with it."

Nettle let her gaze fall away. "It's done now... And it's right. It's what Doc always wanted. What he dreamt of. Why we were developing other areas. No one can feel safe if we're divided."

"Maybe," I said. "But I was only thinking of myself. What *I* wanted."

She swivelled her eyes a little. I could see her looking at me from their corners.

I dropped my gaze. "I told Tun today that the Masu had taught me what it meant to be human, but I think I still have a long way to go."

Nettle snorted softly, and looked into the distance again. "I think we all do."

"Yeah," I said, then stood upright, took her hand, faced her. "But we can do it together, right?"

She turned her whole head this time, searching my eyes for something. Said nothing.

I squirmed inside. Licked my lips. "If you don't... want to do it to-gether... I'll understand," I stammered. "I really blew it, I know. But I love you, Nettle. I do. And I'm ready to stop taking—and give."

She still stared at me.

My palms began to feel sweaty. I could feel my heart wringing itself inside out. My throat constricted. Why wasn't she saying anything?

"I'll get out of your life if you want me to," I forced out. "Just liaise, deal with all the crap, whatever you need, but... but I don't think I can navigate this alone."

I couldn't think of anything worse than losing her after everything we'd been through, but I had to be fair to her. Had to stop presuming.

Nettle glanced down, then after a long pause, lifted her face to me, and her mouth twisted into a wry smile. "Have I ever left you alone in my valley?"

Relieved beyond belief, I snorted. "You never left me alone because you didn't trust me!" I turned serious, reached for her waist, pulled her closer. "Do you trust me now?"

Her face closed over again, and I waited in agony while the moment stretched. Then a soft smile broke upon her lips, clearing away the storm clouds from the rest of her face.

"With my life," she said.

I smiled, letting out a thankful breath, then wrapped my other arm around her shoulders and drew her into an embrace, resting my head against hers.

She pressed in, creeping her hand up my chest till it rested over my heart.

I drew back a little, stroked her cheek. "I'm gonna live up to that trust," I said. "I promise."

"You better," she teased, her dark, liquid eyes turning playful. "Or Shana might eat you."

I let out a laugh. "Nah, she'd feed me to a giant striax python."

Nettle smiled, circling her fingers at the base of my throat. "How very fitting," she agreed with a laugh, then looked down and sighed. "I need to be a little more generous, don't I? A little less... prickly?"

I lifted her chin. "Those prickles always guarded a rose."

She blinked away sudden moisture. "That might just be the nicest thing anyone's ever said to me."

"Glad I was the one who got to say it then."

There was silence as we gazed at each other, and my heart began to pound, then scream with longing. I loved this woman so much, but I was so glad I didn't get to kiss her as soon as we'd landed. That we'd talked first. If we hadn't, I would have stolen that kiss, not given it. Now it would be more real, more mutual—just like a mind-link connection. I would reach out, and she would reach back, and we'd catch each other. Partner.

My voice came out husky. "So... can I kiss you now? Properly?"

The hand at my throat drifted down the buttons on my shirt, then stole around to my back, adding pressure. My stomach swam, and my chest tingled as the soft smile on her face returned, more radiant this time. "I'd like that... Miyu."

With no further encouragement, I slid splayed fingers into her hair and leaned forward, then, just like Shana, gently forged a connection, my lips brushing hers. Slowly, deliberately, unhurried by desire and so, so grateful, I made each soft pull on her lips an opportunity to show her how precious she was. This was not the rushed euphoria of victory, but the lingering tenderness of commitment, and I wanted to be fully present for every achingly beautiful moment of it.

The kiss was richer, deeper, than the one we'd shared earlier, and I savoured each head tilt, each whisper of breath, each butterfly brush of skin.

Nettle had longed to be safe, but the valley wouldn't be her only haven anymore. I would be too, and I let her know that through the gentle strength of my arms, and the tender caresses of hands determined to soothe and heal all her wounded places.

The burst of warmth in my chest wasn't about me anymore, it was about us, and for the first time in my life, I knew true contentment. Nothing more was needed than what we had here.

There would be no scarcity anymore.

Only abundance.

That knowledge would allow me to be human, and I vowed then and there to spend the rest of my life learning what that really meant.

Author's Note

I BEGAN WRITING AT one of the lowest points in my life. Being a wife and mother to four had completely drained me, and I felt more like a husk than a person, existing only to meet other people's needs. I had forgotten what it felt like to be *me*, and lived under a cloud of depression most of the time.

Enter my eldest daughter (14 at the time) with a new Dungeons and Dragons hyperfixation. She asked if we could all play as a family, and my drowning self took a little gulp of air. That game was a life-line. A tiny spark of happiness in my life.

After a few months of play, I made a spur-of-the-moment decision to chronicle our game play. I didn't want to forget this. The laughs. The craziness. The diabolical dice rolls.

And then I found it—joy.

For the first time in more than a decade, I actually felt joy. And I reconnected with who I was as a person. In the tens of thousands of words that poured out, I also began processing my woundedness and found a path to healing.

So I kept going.

The first competition I won paid for a series of editing calls, and my first royalty check paid our power bill for the month. Peanuts. But writing had reawakened my soul, and so now I pour it out for you.

If this book touched you in any way, it would mean the world to me to hear it. Every single review—even if it's just a sentence or two—makes a difference, and I regularly read them.

You can share your thoughts on Goodreads, Amazon, BookBub, or the retailer of your choice—or reach out to me personally via <u>email</u> or <u>social media</u>.

Then go tell a friend about it, so their world can be made a little brighter too.

Share your thoughts on <u>Goodreads</u>.
Let other <u>Amazon</u> customers know this book is worth their time.

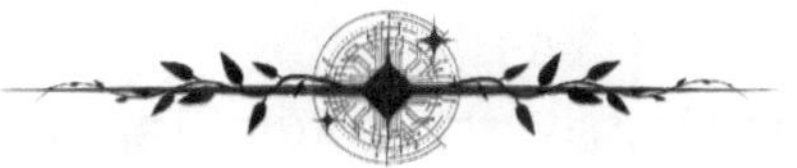

STAY IN TOUCH

To find out when more of our books are coming out, be sure to <u>join our newsletter</u>, *The Slow Readers Society of Eclecta Perennial*, and follow us on Instagram <u>@_eclecta_perennial_books</u> or on Facebook at <u>Eclecta Perennial</u>.

Find out more: <u>https://eclectaperennial.com</u>

Also by Cathryn deVries

Not Ready to Leave Osivirius?

For a behind-the-scenes look at the art and inner workings of *Son of Osivirius*, head to https://eclectaperennial.com/landers/free-bonus-content-offer to get these *exclusive, FREE* guides. You'll be in story nerd heaven!

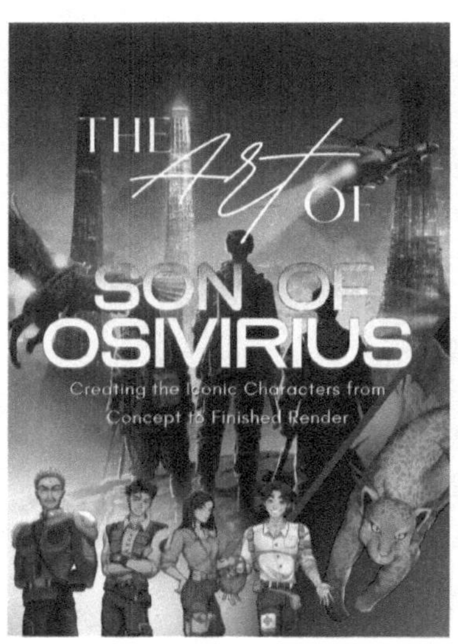

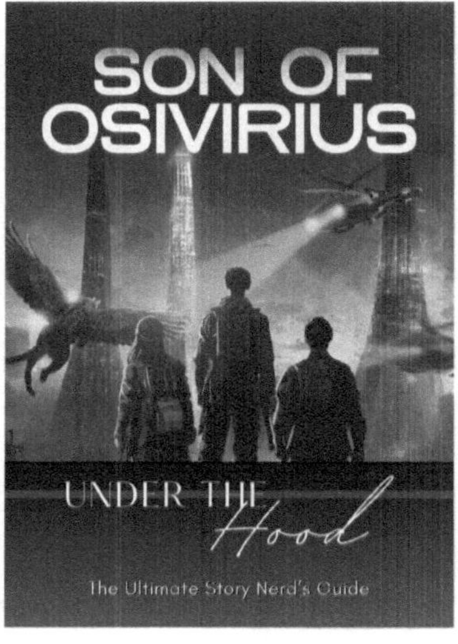

FREE BOOKS

GET A NON-SPOILER 'EPILOGUE' FOR MY ROMANTIC FANTASY TRILOGY FREE!

Ever felt like you didn't quite fit in? Like you were caught between worlds? Too much for one, not enough for the other?

When Tana comes home from a life-changing quest, everything seems rosy at first—until the glamour wears off. Now she just wants to feel like she belongs again, and fixes on winning the title of 'Lightning Hunter' to do just that. But when she finds an orphaned hargryph in amongst the motherlode of lightning cap mushrooms, she must decide what's most important to her—fitting in with the other gnomes, or following her conscience.

Perfect for fans of the fantasy of JRR Tolkien and Brandon Sanderson

AWARD-WINNING ROMANTIC FANTASY

A slave. A tarqin. A hunting cat that knows better than them both.

When Samah is tasked with collecting reeds, she expects only a day of relief from her monotonous and somewhat lonely duties as a slave in Tarquin N'Khapha's library, but when a fey hunting cat catches her attention, possibilities much wilder than that are awakened, for the cat's master needs her help—and maybe something more.

An extraordinary story.

- Dr Rashida Murphy, 2023 Stuart and Hadow judge on awarding 1st place.

ADDITIONAL RESOURCES

Would you like to introduce your Book Club to *Son of Osivirius*? Then why not download my FREE book club guide? The PDF is available from https://eclectaperennial.com/pages/bonus-material

Are you a high school educator? *Son of Osivirius* could make a great addition to your English curriculum. This comprehensive educators guide is also available FREE from https://eclectaperennial.com/pages/bonus-material.

ACKNOWLEDGEMENTS

No work of fiction is created in isolation, and without the following people, this book would be a shadow of itself. Firstly, I need to thank my daughters, Emalyn and Aleria. They never fail to let me know when my writing is boring, lacklustre or cringy. Conversely, they are also my greatest cheerleaders, and have used their artistic talents in support of my writing, particularly the Kickstarter edition of this book.

Next, I'd like to thank my critique partner, Tyler K for reading my very rough and much shorter first draft and sparking the idea to add Nettle's POV. I can't even imagine the book without it now. I'd also like to thank my beta readers Tyler (again), Hannah G, Stephen H, Addison H, Kathryn J, Ben L, and Jemma P. Your feedback was invaluable in revising the next-to-final draft, and I hope you notice the many changes inspired by your honest, thoughtful (and sometimes hard to take) feedback.

I must also thank my developmental editor, Alice Sudlow. As always, Alice, you are *amazing* to work with and made the story so much richer with your probing questions and story expertise.

Alongside Alice, I also wish to thank Shawn Coyne and Tim Grahl of *The Story Grid*. Your work helped me understand story structure in a way that was both objective and transcendent. I love how your mind works, Shawn. Plus, you trained Alice.

To my line editor, Kim Smith: thank you. Not just for your wonderful editing, but for your support and belief in me, and for just being a fabulous person.

Thanks a million to my artist @alfibunneni! You brought my characters to life, and I am forever grateful. You are an absolute pleasure to work with, and we have to do this again sometime!

To the crew at 100 Covers, you nailed it. Thanks for my beautiful cover.

I also want to thank my street team and everyone in the Kickstarter for Authors Facebook group. I couldn't have got this story into so many hands without you! Some of you were friends, but many of you were complete strangers. I am amazed by your generous spirits!

Thank you also to my Kickstarter backers for believing in me and this book.

To my friends and family, thank you for your encouragement and for giving me the space to write.

And finally, I must thank the Beloved Trinity, for without you, there would be no story to tell.

ABOUT THE AUTHOR

Cathryn deVries is a recovering perfectionist and award-winning fantasy and sci-fi author who has been going slowly (or rapidly?) insane over fifteen years of home-schooling her four children, two of whom are on the autism spectrum. A former Air Force engineer, she now explores themes of restorative justice, empowerment, connection with earth and spirit, and finding the true self in her work—all wrapped up in an epic package of immersive world-building and sweet romance.

With her neurodiverse daughter Emalyn, she has co-written a romantic epic fantasy trilogy that fans of Brandon Sanderson and J.R.R. Tolkien will feel right at home in. She and her family live in the Gold Coast Hinterland of Australia, where she enjoys living in a rainforest and pretending she's an elf.